A Loose End

David Morsilli

Marianne,

Seldom is the truth found
on the surface,
So glad you enjoyed the read.

David Morsilli

ISBN: 0692825185
ISBN 13: 9780692825181
Library of Congress Control Number: 2016921195
David Morsilli, Providence, RI

To all those who have found the courage to pursue their dreams.

There is only one thing that makes a dream impossible to achieve: the fear of failure.

—Paul Coelho, *The Alchemist*

Special thanks to Lynn and her amazing team at Seven Stars Bakery on Hope Street in Providence, where the best coffee and the most delicious bread and pastries in Rhode Island are served. It was at Seven Stars Bakery that I spent most mornings for the past several years writing this novel.

And ye shall know the truth and the truth shall make you free.

—John VIII-XXXII. This biblical verse is etched into the wall of the original CIA building.

The best argument against democracy is a five-minute conversation with the average voter.

—Winston Churchill

Part 1

1

EVERYTHING ABOUT THE woman stood out against the back-drop of the frenzied lunchtime crowd. The restaurant was located at the edge of Rockefeller Center on Forty-Eighth Street, between Fifth and Sixth Avenues, a few blocks from Times Square, the pulse of Manhattan. It was two weeks before the holidays, and the city was getting its first snowfall of the year. Au Bon Pain was packed to capacity with a mix of tourists and low- to midlevel professionals. This woman was neither.

There was a seriousness about her presence. She was sitting alone at a table for two, facing the entrance, not eating, and seemingly with no intention of eating. She had a slender frame and sat with her back upright, her shoulders back, and her head in perfect alignment over her hips. Her hands rested in her lap, and her legs were crossed, right knee draped over the left. Her dignified posture exuded confidence without pretense.

She had straight, brownish-blond hair that fell about eight inches below her shoulders. From where I was standing in line while waiting to order lunch, about fifteen feet away and diagonally behind her to the left, I could only observe the profile of her face. Her cheekbones, nose, chin, and jawline were proportionate and slightly angular, as if sculpted from clay, not chiseled from stone. Her skin was white but not pale. It didn't appear that she was wearing any makeup, but if she was, there may have been the slightest detection of mascara and lipstick. I was curious about the color of her eyes, but I couldn't see them from my vantage point.

She was no more than thirty years old but with a refined sophistication that was beyond her years. Her clothes were likely from an exclusive department store such as Bergdorf Goodman—or perhaps from one of the European clothing boutiques on the Upper East Side. She wore a three-quarter-length light-beige coat, most likely cashmere, but there was no way to know for certain without touching. The coat was still buttoned, and the hem rested just above her knees while she was sitting. It was her brown leather boots that made the outfit. They rose above her calves and stopped slightly below her bare knees. The heels were two, maybe three, inches. There was a richness to the contrasting earth tones of the brown boots and beige coat. Her look, beauty, and style were timeless in every sense.

I was on a lunch break from my sales job when I saw this woman. There could have been ten thousand people in the restaurant, and I still would have noticed her. It was as if I was meant to see her. From the instant I saw her, there was no escaping the gravitational pull of her presence. As stunningly beautiful as she was, that wasn't what drew my attention to her. There was something else. I was certain I didn't know the woman, and yet there was something disarmingly familiar about her.

Despite the turmoil and fluidity of the fast-paced lunchtime crowd, the woman sat undistracted in her own quiet space at her table. Her calmness and sense of purpose were entirely incongruous with the surroundings. The question begged, why was she there?

The moment I posed this question to myself, the woman slightly stirred in her chair. Her posture stiffened, and she began to anxiously rub her hands as if applying hand cream while simultaneously unfolding her legs. For that brief moment, her veil of poised calm had lifted, but she quickly regained her composure. Curious as to what provoked this reaction, my eyes followed hers to the front entrance, where there stood a man who had just entered the restaurant. The man was approximately sixty years old. He wore a long black overcoat over a dark suit and tie. His outfit looked to be about two sizes too big, giving a somewhat disheveled appearance. The man's appearance was distinctly Russian. His face was roundish, not angular, and his skin was pale with a faint yellow hue. He had a full head of dark-brown hair, too dark for his age. His eyes were gray and slightly almond shaped, one of the physical traits leftover from the Mongol invaders of Russia in the thirteenth century.

As the man stood near the doorway, he casually wiped the snow off his left shoulder with his right hand. He feigned indifference to his surroundings, but then, in a deliberate movement, he raised his eyes and made eye contact with the woman. They exchanged the most ever-so-subtle head gestures to acknowledge each other's presence. In that instant, I knew something was happening. I had the presence of mind to avert my eyes in order to continue watching them through the reflection in the large mirror that extended along the length of the side wall. This man then looked to his right shoulder, and while brushing the snow with his left hand, his eyes scanned the entire crowd.

Satisfied that nobody was watching, he approached the woman's table. He remained standing as they exchanged a few words, neither betraying any emotion. The woman reached into her handbag and withdrew her wallet, opening it to reveal her driver's license, which was in a laminated sleeve. She handed the opened wallet to the man, and he studied her license, first looking back and forth from the picture to the woman. Then with his index finger, he scanned the biographical information on her license. Once he was confident she was his contact, he handed the wallet back to her, and she replaced it in her handbag. He then reached into the left inside pocket of his overcoat and removed a slightly bulging brown manila-type envelope that measured about six inches by nine inches. With outstretched arms the woman held out her handbag, and he placed the envelope inside.

I looked at the nearby tables to see if anyone else had just witnessed what I saw, but to my surprise, nobody was aware that anything had just transpired. It never ceases to amaze me just how oblivious people are to their surroundings, only immersed in their own little worlds.

My attention returned to the man and woman. They exchanged a few parting words, and then he exited the restaurant and turned left onto Forty-Eighth Street, walking west toward Times Square. The mystery woman watched the man through the plate-glass window until he was out of view. She remained for another ten seconds and then exited the restaurant in the opposite direction, toward Fifth Avenue.

2

ADOLF HITLER EMERGED on the political scene in Germany during the tumultuous years following the country's humiliating defeat in the Great War, which we now know as World War I. The war lasted from 1914 to 1918 and pitted the Central powers of Germany, the Austro-Hungarian Empire, Bulgaria, and Turkey (Ottoman Empire) against the Allied powers consisting of Great Britain, France, Russia, Italy (entered 1915), and the United States (entered 1917).

In defeat, and identified as the aggressor, Germany was forced to accept the punitive terms and conditions set forth by the Allies in the Treaty of Versailles, which formally ended the war on June 28, 1919. The treaty placed responsibility for the war squarely on Germany for its leadership role in a war that caused an estimated seventeen million deaths and unimaginable destruction across Europe. Under the terms of the treaty, Germany was obligated to relinquish all overseas colonial possessions; handover some of its territory to neighboring countries; make staggering war-reparation payments to the Allies (primarily France); disarm its military to the point of giving it no offensive capabilities; and refrain from manufacturing any military weapons, including planes and vehicles. The Germans were humiliated by the terms and conditions of the treaty, but Germany had no choice but to sign.

Germans had always been a proud, extremely well-educated, and culturally rich people whose history reached back two thousand years. However, the political vacuum and economic turmoil that characterized the postwar years put the German population in such a disgraced state of being. It was this low point that made the population vulnerable to the charismatic rantings of Adolf Hitler. Hitler appealed to the population's nostalgia when he spoke of restoring Germany's pride and returning the country to its former glory. He promised, if elected, his first order of business would be to disband the country's stifling obligations under the Treaty of Versailles. Hitler understood the importance of well-crafted propaganda that resonated with the lowest common denominator of the population to achieve political ends. "All propaganda has to be popular and has to accommodate itself to the comprehension of the least intelligent of those whom it seeks to reach," Adolf Hitler had said.

Hitler's fiercely nationalist message steadily gained momentum. In the German Reichstag (parliament) election of November 6, 1932, his National Socialist German Worker's Party (NSDAP), better known as the Nazi Party, came in first place with a 33 percent plurality of the votes. This election victory opened the door for the German president, Paul von Hindenburg, who, under the German constitution, shared power with the Reichstag, to appoint Adolf Hitler chancellor of the Reichstag on January 30, 1933.

Less than a month later, on the night of February 27, a mysterious fire destroyed the Reichstag building. Adolf Hitler immediately placed responsibility for the fire on the communists, whom he despised and viewed as the Nazi Party's main political rival. Preying on the population's distress, Hitler fanned the flames of fear and disinformation, declaring that Germany was on the verge of a communist revolution. Hitler told the population that to counter this domestic threat from within, decisive and strong action would need to be taken to save Germany from its enemies.

Within twenty-four hours of the Reichstag fire, Hitler drafted the Emergency Reichstag Fire Decree, which he then convinced the ailing eighty-five-year-old President von Hindenburg to ratify, thus making it constitutional. The emergency decree declared a national emergency, which allowed Hitler and the Nazi Party to suspend civil liberties for the entire population; ban the private ownership of guns; take control of the free press to ensure there was unilateral pro-Nazi reporting; and most significant, arrest not only communists but any political opponents or anyone who voiced any opposition whatsoever to the Nazi Party.

With the Nazi Party's political opponents under arrest, dissent was eliminated. Hitler then drafted the Enabling Act, which granted him the administrative and legislative powers that would allow him to rule by decree during a national emergency. President von Hindenburg, by then on his deathbed, once again acquiesced to Hitler's demands and ratified the Enabling Act.

The Reichstag fire, along with the emergency decrees that followed, allowed Adolf Hitler and the Nazi Party to seize absolute control of the German government. Virtually overnight, Germany went from being a democracy to a totalitarian state renamed the Third Reich, to which Adolf Hitler named himself führer. This was the ultimate power play. Adolf Hitler knew, as many leaders and governments know, that the most expedient way to consolidate or usurp political power from within is to capitalize on any threat to national security, whether real, imagined, or fabricated, in order to manipulate the population into freely giving up their civil liberties (freedoms and privacy), all in the name of restoring security.

Convinced that Hitler had saved the country from a communist revolution, a feverish nationalistic fervor swept across the population, which served to unite the country squarely behind Adolf Hitler. It is widely believed that the Reichstag fire was a classic "false-flag operation," orchestrated by Adolf Hitler and the Nazi inner circle. A false-flag operation is when an act of some sort is carried out by one group but made to appear as if it was perpetrated by another group, for political or military gain. Hitler was neither the first nor the last to manipulate events in order to achieve a desired result.

Under the Third Reich, the country turned into a police state under a newly created "secret" police organization named the Gestapo. With a vast network of surveillance and informants, the Gestapo was able to monitor and maintain tight totalitarian control over the population through the use of terror and the threat that at any time the secret police could arrest and imprison anyone without trial.

An armed wing of the Nazi Party was also established and named the Schutzstaffel, better known by its "SS" abbreviation. The SS was headed by Heinrich Himmler and was designed to be a standalone organization, separate from the Wehrmacht (German armed forces) and government. Nazism was basically racist nationalism, and the SS were responsible for the racial policy of the Third Reich. Members were chosen based on Aryan racial purity who exemplified an "Aryan master race." The SS were the most fanatical believers of the Nazi ideology and had sworn an oath of loyalty to Adolf Hitler and the Nazi cause until death.

The real power of the Third Reich resided in the Ministry of Public Enlightenment and Propaganda. It was this ministry that ensured the German public only had access to Nazi-generated propaganda. News from any other source was banned. Absolute editorial control was maintained over newspapers, magazines, literature, music, radios, and art, among others. This ministry also organized Hitler rallies in specially constructed arenas around the country that could hold half a million people. These political and military events included marching bands and lots of flag waving, all the things that are designed to instill a sense of nationalism to restore German pride, while at the same time, these events served the purpose of creating a cult-like status around Adolf Hitler. "The essence of propaganda consists in winning people over to an idea so sincerely, so vitally, that in the end they succumb to it utterly and can never escape from it," said Josef Goebbels, minister of Public Enlightenment and Propaganda.

The Third Reich demonstrated how a well-developed propaganda campaign of simple slogans and images were more effective than any weapon in the manipulation and subjugation of an entire population. The repeated theme was always to appeal to the nationalism of the people, which in the Balkans nationalism is known as the ugly cousin of patriotism. The Nazis directed and controlled everything from politics, economy, business, education, and the military.

While the Third Reich was readying for war, the rest of Europe, still reeling from the death and destruction from the Great War, coupled with the worldwide depression that followed in 1929, was too distracted to notice that Germany, in violation of the terms set out under the Treaty of Versailles, had rebuilt its military war machine. Hitler, with the country solidly behind him, was now in a position to not only restore German pride after his country's shameful defeat in World War I but also to avenge the humiliating terms and conditions imposed on Germany by the Allied powers under the Treaty of Versailles.

What the world could have never imagined though, and still hasn't realized over seventy years later, was that the impending World War II and the horrors that the world would come to known as the Holocaust were merely smokescreens designed to distract the world's attention away from Adolf Hitler's secret plot against America, which would eventually clear the path for his dream of a "Thousand Year Reich" to become a reality. "All warfare is based on deception," Sun Tzu said in *The Art of War.*

3

MY FIRST IMPULSE was to get out of line and follow the woman. I had so many unanswered questions. Who was this mystery woman? What was in the envelope? Where was she going? Who was the man? I've read many spy novels in my years and knew that my overactive imagination was getting out way ahead of me.

To further complicate matters, the eerie feeling persisted that there was something familiar about the mystery woman, or something. Whatever the feeling was, now that the mystery woman had exited the restaurant, I was being strangely pulled to follow her.

Under normal circumstances, it would have been easy to talk myself out of taking up pursuit. I had spent the entire morning preparing a PowerPoint presentation for a two o'clock sales meeting, which was less than an hour away. The truth of the matter was I didn't even understand why I cared about the meeting because I hated my job. I never imagined that at the age of thirty-one I'd be doing something as uninteresting and unfulfilling as selling corporate voice-messaging systems. Only a few years earlier, I was determined to follow my own path overseas, but none of my plans materialized. If that wasn't disappointing enough, I was two years into a personal relationship that had run its course pretty much from the outset. The last few years had taken almost everything out of me. I wanted a new life but just couldn't muster the strength or courage to make the necessary changes. My situation, both professional and personal, was smothering my spirit a little more with each passing day.

I needed change in my life, and this mystery woman provided the perfect opportunity. *Her presence was an omen of sorts*, I thought. My intuition, which the spiritual types will say is our soul talking to us, was very clearly telling me to follow the woman. There was something to be learned, or something. I could feel it.

This low point in my life served to embolden me to make the uncharacteristic decision to follow. A little spontaneity was exactly what I needed. What's the worst that can happen? With that thought, I threw caution to the wind and got out of line to follow her.

As I made my way to the door, determined to follow this woman, I could sense something wasn't right. I couldn't put a finger on it, but my sixth sense, which I've learned to trust, was telling me that danger was lurking.

4

DURING ADOLF HITLER'S rise to power in Germany, he was closely aligned with America's elite. The closest thing America has to an aristocracy are the white Anglo-Saxon Protestants (WASPs). Historically, the WASPs represented "old money" and were the ones who held a disproportionate amount of financial, political, and social power and influence in America. The WASPs, also known as Blue Bloods, were considered the backbone of America. They were the doers; they were the intellectuals, industrialists, and Wall Street bankers. These were America's elite, and they knew full well how to wield their immense power discreetly, behind the scenes, in both elected and appointed positions throughout the government. The Blue Bloods were the establishment in America, and their agenda always had a way of becoming America's agenda, at home and abroad. The Blue Bloods were America's ruling class. The Blue Bloods are America's shadow government.

At the time Adolf Hitler surfaced in the early 1920s, the greatest threat to America's elite had come several years earlier when, in 1917, Vladimir Lenin led the successful communist-inspired Bolshevik Revolution, which overthrew the Romanov Dynasty in Russia. From that point on, America's elite believed that the greatest threat to their capitalist way of life in the United States was the danger posed by the Soviet Union.

There was no other political or economic ideology more diametrically opposed to, and in conflict with, capitalism as was communism. In simple terms, American capitalist society was democratic, citizens had guaranteed individual rights and freedoms, there was private ownership of the means of production, privately owned property was allowed, and freedom of enterprise was the way of life. Under the communist system in the Soviet Union, the government was totalitarian—meaning the state has total authority, the citizens did not have guaranteed individual rights and freedoms, there is public (not private) ownership of the means of production, privately owned property was prohibited, and freedom of enterprise was banned.

Thus, when Adolf Hitler emerged onto Germany's political scene in the early 1920s, spewing his vitriolic hatred of communists, America's capitalist elite not only welcomed Hitler's presence, but they also gave generously to his political campaigns. In the eyes of the US government and America's elite, Hitler was exactly the counterbalance needed to stem the spread of communism across Europe, which had already started taking root among some of Europe's intellectuals.

Adolf Hitler's talk of a "master race" brought America's elite even closer to the Nazis because that talk had been circulating among the aristocratic class in Great Britain and with America's Blue Bloods ever since Charles Darwin published his seminal work, *The Origin of Species*, in 1859. Back then these discussions were known as the "eugenics movement," which was about improving the gene pool through selective breeding in order to eliminate the world's inferior races. In a nutshell, Nazism, also known as National Socialism, can be described as socialized Darwinism. This talk of superior and inferior gene pools appealed to the aristocratic class everywhere because it allowed them to rationalize and justify their own "evolutionary superiority."

Adolf Hitler's opinion of America was mixed. On one hand, Hitler viewed the United States as a mongrel nation that lacked racial purity and that its democracy wrongfully served to empower the minorities. He was convinced that this melting-pot experiment, along with the unrestrained and overindulgent nature of America's flavor of capitalism, would ultimately lead to the country's demise. On the other hand, Hitler was in awe of the sheer scale of America's industrial base and growth potential, which dwarfed Germany's. This, Hitler knew, was America's greatest strength and was what enabled the country to project its unparalleled military power and political influence around the globe.

When Adolf Hitler seized power in 1933, there was an all-out effort to grow Germany's industrial base in order to put people back to work and take the country out of its economic slump and become a thriving economy. In addition, it would also provide Hitler with the revenues needed to militarize the Third Reich. The only way this accelerated rate of growth could occur was if there was a massive infusion of foreign capital. America's financiers on Wall Street had been investing in German companies since the economic turmoil of the mid-1920s, so it came as no surprise that he turned to his American capitalist friends for help. Hitler knew that America's capitalists, many of whom were derisively called the Robber Barons of the late nineteenth and early twentieth centuries due to their unscrupulous business practices, would have no qualms in preparing the Third Reich for war as long as there were generous profits to be made.

Some of America's most powerful corporations and banks came to the aid of Hitler's Third Reich: Standard Oil (Rockefeller), Ford Motors (Henry Ford), General Motors (JP Morgan), General Electric,

International Telephone and Telegraph (ITT), DuPont, Coca-Cola, Metro-Goldwyn-Mayer, Dow Chemical, Woolworth, Alcoa Aluminum (Mellon), IBM, Kodak, Nestlé, JP Morgan, Chase Bank, and Citibank, among countless others. In some cases these corporations and banks made capital investments into German corporations, and in other situations American companies expanded their own manufacturing operations into corporate-friendly Germany, usually in partnership with their German sister corporations.

The contributions of America's corporations to the Third Reich's war machine were enormous: Rockefeller's Standard Oil, in partnership with the German corporation IG Farben, built massive oil refineries that were essential for the Nazi war machine. Because Germany had limited oil reserves, it was dependent on imported oil, the supply of which could be easily disrupted during a time of war. As a solution to this problem, Standard Oil shared its top-secret patents with IG Farben, allowing the Nazis to develop synthetic oil from coal (Germany had massive coal reserves). Ford Motor Company and General Motors established subsidiaries in Germany that manufactured tanks and military vehicles. General Electric, in partnership with its German equivalent, AEG, built power plants to supply electricity throughout the country. IBM manufactured the Hollerith punch-card machines that allowed the SS to manage all the resources necessary to carry out the Holocaust. The examples of America's corporations helping Hitler would fill many books.

Hitler also urged German corporations to expand abroad, primarily to the United States: IG Farben, Heche, Krupp, Volkswagen, BMW, Siemens, Daimler-Mercedes Benz, BASF, and Bayer, among nearly two hundred others. In some cases these corporations grew their operations, and in other cases they simply bought stock in American corporations for equity ownership. Hitler's rationale for this was that German corporations would be able to send profits back to the Fatherland to provide additional capital to fund the Third Reich.

The relationships between American and German corporations were mired in partnerships, patent sharing, holding companies, and outright capital investments for equity stakes in one another's corporations. This cross-pollination of investments between corporations blurred the lines of national ownership, which continues to this day.

Hitler understood the nature of America's corporations, and all corporations for that matter, was that their greed transcended national loyalties. These corporations are truly global entities and know no boundaries, physical, moral, or otherwise, as long as there are profits to be made. "Merchants have no country," Thomas Jefferson said.

Hitler had long identified America's corporations as the country's greatest strength. What he also knew was that unlike Germany and other fascist countries, where the government was in control of the corporations, in America it was the corporations, not the people, who truly controlled the US government and the political system. "Somewhere there is a gap in his armor, a weakness that can be attacked instead," the ancient Chinese military stratagem suggests.

5

THE INSTANT I opened the door to exit the restaurant, the frigid wind hit my face and filled my lungs. The cold has a way of awakening all my senses. I always feel more alive and alert in the dead of winter than I do during any other season. As I hurried to catch up to the mystery woman, I caught a glimpse of the ten-story Christmas tree on display in Rockefeller Plaza. *What a beautiful time of year to be in Manhattan*, I thought.

As I hurried toward Fifth Avenue, dodging pedestrians on the crowd-filled sidewalk, my eyes darted ahead for the mystery woman, who had about a five- to seven-second head start. It took only a few seconds to spot her desert-sand-colored coat, with her hair kicking wildly in the wind. She was about thirty feet ahead, so I increased my pace to close the gap.

The wind gusts were so strong that day, more so than usual. In metropolitan cities there is a phenomenon known as the urban-canyon effect. This occurs as a result of the disturbance of the airflow between uneven and tightly clustered buildings, which results in fierce gusts of wind.

The stimuli in Manhattan are everywhere. As focused as I was, much like in Pavlov's experiment, my olfactory nodes reacted to the smell of honey-roasted peanuts at a nearby vending cart. The peanuts were roasted using sugar, honey, and a dash of vanilla. The vanilla is the secret ingredient that gives the peanuts that saliva-tingling aroma that one never forgets.

As I drew to within fifteen feet of the woman, I wasn't expecting to witness anything, which was why I didn't realize anything happened until it was too late. A man approached from the opposite direction—a different man than the one inside the restaurant. He wore a dark overcoat buttoned all the way to his neck, with a black fedora tilted downward, with the brim covering his eyes. At the last instant, he deliberately stepped into the mystery woman's path, with his left hand slightly raised, and nonchalantly yet purposefully collided with her. He may have even whispered something into her ear. She managed to take just one more step forward, then in slow motion, she went into a descending three-quarter spiral turn and collapsed onto the slush-covered cement sidewalk.

I froze in place, stunned by what I had just witnessed. Several bystanders franticly surrounded her, wanting to help but not knowing what to do. One of them yelled out, asking if anyone knew CPR. Another voice yelled that he was calling 911.

Amid the chaos of the scene, I watched in disbelief as the man wearing the fedora casually squatted next to the mystery woman's handbag, slipped his hand inside, and then removed the manila envelope that she had received only minutes earlier. With envelope in hand, he stood, but before walking away, he locked eyes with me. I'll never forget those eyes. He had the coldest ice-blue eyes I had ever seen. They were the eyes of a killer. I knew in that instant that the mystery woman was dead. His laser-beam stare bore down on me for two, maybe three, seconds before he broke eye contact, pivoted, and, with a distinct cadence, dissolved into the crowd. Just like that, I became "a loose end."

6

BY 1938 THE Third Reich was gearing up to be the aggressor in a second Europe-wide war. The first signs of an outwardly resurgent Germany came on March 12, 1938, when the Wehrmacht (German armed forces), on friendly terms, occupied and then annexed its close ally Austria. The following year the Wehrmacht retook the former German territory of the Sudetenland province (whose population was German), which had been surrendered to Czechoslovakia under the Treaty of Versailles. Within a year the Wehrmacht went on to occupy the entire country. Great Britain and France did not protest Hitler's actions at this time, as they preferred a policy of "appeasement" toward the Third Reich, which basically entailed looking the other way as to avoid any direct conflict.

During this time Adolf Hitler's speeches at home began to take on a more nationalistic racist tone, which placed an increased emphasis on the Aryan master race. He also took the opportunity to ratchet up the anti-Semitic propaganda by claiming that communism, which he detested, was a Jewish conspiracy that sought world domination. Laws were passed that made life unbearable for the Jews: banned from public places, not allowed to own their own businesses, prevented from working, and other hardships. The Nazis propagated a virulent, cruel hatred for the Jewish population. Events took an ominous turn on the night of November 9-10, 1938. This night would become known as Kristallnacht, which translates as the "night of broken glass." Ordinary Germans, organized by Nazi officials, rampaged through the entire country, destroying and setting on fire Jewish-owned homes, buildings, businesses, and synagogues. Kristallnacht foreshadowed the events to come for the Jewish population of Europe.

Seemingly in pursuit of the military domination of Europe, Hitler then targeted Poland. Wanting to make it appear that Poland was the aggressor, the SS concocted a false-flag operation known as the Gleiwitz incident, in which SS soldiers, donning Polish military uniforms, attacked a German radio station along their shared border. Hitler then used this charade as the pretext for the invasion of Poland the next day, September 1, 1939. Treaty obligations with Poland then committed both Great Britain and France to then declare war on Germany, leading to the outbreak of World War II.

Europe was in no position to put up much of any resistance to a militarized Third Reich. After invading Poland, with the German efficiency for which the Nazis were known, they swept across Western Europe with blitzkrieg (lightning quick) speed, overwhelming, defeating, then occupying country after country: Denmark and Norway (April 1940), France (May 1940), and the Benelux countries of Luxembourg, Netherlands, and Belgium (May 1940).

During this time, from May 27 to June 4, 1940, there was a curious incident known as the Miracle of Dunkirk. The German Army (Wehrmacht) moved with such overwhelming lightning-quick speed across Western Europe that it caught 340,000 Allied troops (British, French, and Belgian) completely off guard on the coast of France at Dunkirk. The Allied troops had no way of escape and found themselves completely corralled against the coastline by the Wehrmacht.

The German Army could have easily annihilated these Allied soldiers or taken them all as prisoners of war, avoiding the prospect of having to fight them on the battlefield at a later date. However, in what has been one of the many mysteries to emerge from the war, Hitler ordered the Wehrmacht not to attack the Allied troops. This reprieve, which has never been understood, allowed Great Britain to organize the largest flotilla in history across the English Channel to rescue the defenseless soldiers. On the surface, Hitler's decision defied logic, especially given his next move.

The Third Reich's next military objective was to invade the island nation of Great Britain. Before the Wehrmacht's amphibious invasion force could be launched across the English Channel, the Nazis needed control over the skies above Great Britain. From July to October 1940, the German Air Force (Luftwaffe) and the Royal Air Force (RAF) fought a fierce air campaign against one another in the Battle of Britain. The RAF would deliver the Third Reich its first loss of the war. Without control over the skies, and curiously lacking resolve, Hitler abandoned his plans to invade the British Isles.

The beginning of the end for the Third Reich came when Adolf Hitler, against the advice of his generals and despite having signed a nonaggression pact with Stalin at the beginning of the war, made the suicidal decision to invade the Soviet Union. The offensive, launched on June 22, 1941, was named Operation Barbarossa and was the largest invasion force in history, consisting of four million soldiers from Nazi Germany and its Axis allies (Italy, Romania, Hungary, Slovakia, Croatia, and Finland). The plan was simple: annihilate the Soviet military, crush the civilian population, and strip the country of every single cultural artifact.

By the end of the war, a staggering twenty million Soviet soldiers and civilians would be killed and many of the country's industrial centers destroyed by the Nazis. Throughout history Russia has been surrounded by enemies, and because of this the country has extensive experience in defensive warfare. As a result, despite these daunting Soviet losses, in much the same way the Russians were eventually able to repel Napoleon's formidable army in its disastrous invasion of 1812, the Soviets also eventually launched a massive counterattack against the Nazis that allowed them to gain the upper hand against the Third Reich.

By invading the Soviet Union, Adolf Hitler unnecessarily opened up a two-front war, fighting the Soviets in the east and the Americans and British in the west. His actions were considered military suicide and directly led to the defeat of the Third Reich. Four out of every five German soldiers killed during World War II died on the eastern front fighting the Soviets. Up until Operation Barbarossa, the Nazis had demonstrated such sound political and military decisions. Why then would Hitler, only a few months before winter, and against the advice of his generals, unnecessarily draw the Soviet Union into the war?

Hitler's suicidal decision to invade the Soviet Union and opening up a two-front war was considered to be the action of a madman. Nobody could have ever imagined that there was a method to his madness. "Inflict injury on oneself (Germany) to win the enemy's (America) trust. Pretending to be injured has two possible applications. In the first, the enemy (America) is lulled into relaxing his guard since he no longer considers you to be an immediate threat. The second is a way of ingratiating yourself to your enemy (America) by pretending the injury was caused by a mutual enemy (Communist Soviet Union)," says an ancient Chinese military stratagem.

Parallel to waging war in Europe, Heinrich Himmler and the SS were given the responsibility for implementing the Holocaust, which was to be the "final solution" to the "Jewish question." Carrying out the genocide was entrusted to the SS because of their unwavering obedience to Hitler and the Nazi cause. The SS were hardcore, fanatical, and dependable. They could be relied upon to carry out orders under any circumstances. After all, they were the ones who swore an oath of loyalty to Hitler and to the Nazi cause until death. The SS carried out the forced deportations of Jews from occupied countries in Western Europe to the concentration camps. As for Poland and the Soviet Union, the SS deployed the Einsatzgruppen mobile killing units to exterminate those populations. By the time the war ended, the SS had murdered six million Jewish people and another five million Roma (Gypsies), Slavs, Poles, disabled persons, and any others deemed "undesirable" by the Nazis. The Holocaust was organized in a methodical, efficient, and organized manner. It was a truly cold-blooded Nazi operation.

On June 6, 1944, the United States and Great Britain launched the D-Day invasion onto the beaches of Normandy to expel the Nazis from France, Belgium, and the Netherlands and then to advance into German territory for the final push of the war. In an unexpected setback, on December 16, 1944, the Wehrmacht, with four hundred thousand troops and nearly six hundred tanks, in an attempt to retake Belgium, launched a surprise counterattack on 225,000 American troops near the town of Bastogne in the Ardennes Forest in what would come to be known as the Battle of the Bulge. General Patton and the Third Army, which had progressed farther than anyone had expected and was readying to advance into Germany, was diverted to Bastogne to help fellow American soldiers under siege. Eventually the Americans repelled the German attack but not before suffering twenty thousand deaths in combat, making it the bloodiest battle of the war for the Americans in Europe. In yet another mystery to come out of World War II, to this date it's still not known how the Wehrmacht was able to launch such a massive surprise attack on US troops at a time when Great Britain had already broken the Nazis' encrypted Enigma communications.

By January 1945, the Wehrmacht and SS were in full retreat back to the Fatherland, with the Americans and British converging on Germany from the west and the Soviets from the east. On April 30, 1945, Adolf Hitler and Eva Braun were purported to have committed suicide inside an underground bunker. Then it is said that a bodyguard placed their bodies into a bomb crater, doused them with kerosene, and burned their bodies. The only remains ever recovered by the Russians was a charred skull fragment. Decades later this skull fragment would be DNA tested, and it was determined that it belonged to neither Adolf Hitler nor Eva Braun. General Eisenhower (supreme Allied commander) and Josef Stalin both believed that Hitler escaped. Regardless, the official story was that Adolf Hitler was dead by suicide.

A week later on May 8, 1945, Germany unconditionally surrendered to the Allies. When the war ended, Germany was divided up by the Allies into two spheres of influence, as was the capitol of Berlin. The east was occupied by the Soviet Union, and the west was occupied by the United States, Great Britain, and France. This predictably laid the foundation for what would become known as the Cold War confrontation between the capitalist United States and the communist Soviet Union, which conveniently shifted all the attention away from the Nazis, precisely as Adolf Hitler had meticulously planned.

7

AFTER THE MAN with the ice-blue eyes vanished from the scene, my attention returned to the woman. She lay motionless in the middle of the cold, slush-covered cement sidewalk. She was surrounded by a small crowd that watched as a man, on his knees by her side, frantically administered hands-only cardio resuscitation. Someone screamed in a hysterical voice, "Is anyone a doctor!" The man attending to the mystery woman, without missing a beat, yelled to no one in particular, "I am a fucking doctor."

After what seemed an eternity but was likely only a few minutes at most, the doctor stopped the chest compressions. He remained in his knees though, with shoulders slumped and head hanging low. It was clear from the pained look of defeat on his face that the woman was beyond the point of resuscitation.

Amid the chaotic scene, I made my way to the center of the circle of gawkers. When I looked down upon the woman, I understood why the doctor had stopped the chest compressions. Her beautiful brown eyes, sprinkled with specks of gold, were wide open, staring up to the universe, which was obstructed by gray snow clouds. Her eyes were slightly glossed over, and her pupils were dilated. She was clearly dead. My heart sank at this realization. Even in death, she held such a graceful repose. I knelt beside her, opposite the doctor, removed my right winter glove, and gently rubbed the lapel of her coat. The soft silken smoothness of the fabric confirmed that it was cashmere. *Of course she wore cashmere*, I thought. Given the circumstances, the observation seemed so trivial. My eyes surveyed her body for anything that could explain her sudden death. Nothing was amiss, but I was certain that the man with the ice-blue eyes had killed her.

I couldn't help but notice a small Star of David pendant hanging from a thin necklace that had come to rest in the hollow of her throat. It was small, no more than three-quarters of an inch in diameter. I placed the Jewish Star between my thumb and index finger and gently stroked it with my thumb, for no other reason than knowing that it must have been special to her. The pendant was made of a silvery-white metal and showed no signs of tarnishing. For such a small piece, its weight and density seemed disproportionately greater than what I expected, which meant it must have been platinum. There was such a well-worn smoothness to the piece that only comes after many years of wear. *This simple yet elegant pendant, no doubt crafted from an era long past, was timeless, just like this mystery woman*, I thought. There was probably a story behind the piece, but I would likely never know.

With the Star of David pendant still between my fingers, my focus slowly returned to her lifeless eyes. The feeling that we somehow connected or maybe had something in common persisted. It made no sense though. After a long pause, in the faintest of whispers, I asked, "Who are you? What was so important in that envelope for that man to kill you?" I was so lost in thought, not even listening to what anyone around me was saying.

Had this been a movie, this would have been the part when someone would have closed her eyelids using his or her thumb and index finger. There was no way I was going to be the person to close the windows to her soul. I'd leave that for someone else. After taking one last look into her beautiful but lifeless eyes, I placed the pendant back in the hollow of her neck and stood, without saying anything. I made my way past the onlookers. Once clear of the crowd, I found a space on the street between two parked cars where I could gather my thoughts.

The woman was already dead, so I knew there was no way of helping her at this point. My thoughts returned to the man with the ice-cold blue eyes. The way he stared into my eyes worried me. He must have known that I saw everything. It occurred to me that I had to vacate the scene as quickly as possible. Even though the killer saw me, there was no way he could know my identity. As long as I could leave the scene without being followed, he'd never know who I was. *That reasoning seemed logical*, I thought.

The killer had disappeared, walking east toward Fifth Avenue, so I started walking west back toward Rockefeller Center. I cut through the plaza, passing by the monstrosity of a Christmas tree. The plaza was filled with tourists, making it the perfect place to get lost in the crowd. I looked behind to see if anyone was following, but there were way too many people to be able to detect anything out of the ordinary, not that I even knew what to look for. Rather than enter my office building through its main entrance on Fifth Avenue, I ducked into the building using the side entrance located on Fifty-Second Street. Once inside, I went directly to the bank of elevators in the center of the lobby and watched to make sure nobody entered the building behind. Maybe I lost a tail or maybe there never was one; I had no idea.

8

THE MYSTERY WOMAN from Au Bon Pain was twenty-nine-year-old Nathalie Rosenfeld, granddaughter of the late André Rosenfeld. Up until the outbreak of World War II, André was a renowned art dealer who lived in Paris with his family. There he owned an art-and-antiques gallery located on Paris's art-influenced Left Bank. The gallery, which was large enough to be a small museum, had been in his family for several generations. It was expected that when the time came, André would turn over the gallery to his children for future Rosenfeld generations.

However, World War II would change all those plans. Two weeks before the Nazis marched into an undefended Paris on June 14, 1940, André and his family, who had the financial means and a contact at the American Embassy with a weakness for antiques, had miraculously been able to secure the necessary travel documents for the family to emigrate to the United States. However, the terms of travel prevented André from taking any valuables with them, including the family's entire art collection, which amounted to over three hundred pieces. The works consisted of paintings, drawings, sculptures, and other various objects from some of Europe's most talented artists, such as Renoir, Braque, Matisse, Picasso, Ingres, Delacroix, Courbet, Rodin,

Cézanne, Degas, Monet, and Lautrec, among others. The current-day value of the collection would be in excess of an estimated $125 million.

André, like most Europeans, did not trust banks or paper currency. Those with the means took the precautionary measure of converting their hard currency into assets deemed liquid, such as gold and gems, both of which tend to hold their value in times of political or economic crisis. There's an inherent danger in entrusting all one's money and other financial resources to any bank, over which one has no control. This was a hedge against the possibility that one day the banking system could be manipulated, crash, or be seized under some guise, thus leaving depositors penniless. This was why in addition to the art works, André also kept a portion of the family's wealth in gold and diamonds, the current day value of which would be about $10 million.

During the war, the Nazis would carry out a remarkably well-organized looting campaign on a scale that Europe hadn't witnessed since Napoleon Bonaparte's reign from 1799 to 1815. The German Army had created art-protection units called *Kunstschutz*, each of which was headed up by an SS officer. The sole responsibility of these units was to loot anything with any artistic, historical, or monetary value, ranging from currencies, gold bullion and other precious metals, and diamonds and other precious stones to religious artifacts, paintings, sculptures, manuscripts, maps, books, ceramics, carpets, tapestries, lithographs, and everything in between. These items were seized from banks, museums, churches, synagogues, archival institutions, libraries, and private property, among others.

When the Wehrmacht entered Paris, French collaborators led a Kunstschutz unit directly to the Rosenfeld's gallery, where the entire art collection of over three hundred pieces was confiscated. Each piece was catalogued and then put into crates and placed into two railroad cars and transported to Germany. By the end of the war, the

Nazis had shipped back to Germany tens of millions of objects that had been looted from the Nazi-occupied territories across Europe. The most prized of the "trophy art" was intended to be put on display at the planned Führer Museum, which was to be constructed in Hitler's hometown of Linz, Austria. The museum was to be the largest in the world, with over twenty miles of galleries. The gold and diamonds were sent elsewhere.

In the chaotic aftermath of the war, mayhem ensued across occupied Germany. One of the two railroad cars containing the Rosenfeld family's artworks was again looted, and the artworks from that one car were sold off to buyers across Europe and beyond, many for only a small fraction of their true value. The second railroad car simply vanished without a trace. There was speculation that it was hit by an errant bomb during the Allied bombing campaign and blown to smithereens, which would explain why there was no trace. Much of the property looted by the Nazis would never surface again for a whole myriad of reasons. This missing railroad car was just one of countless mysteries to come out of World War II.

When the Rosenfeld family arrived in America in 1940, André, along with his wife and three children, settled in the Jewish community in Crown Heights, Brooklyn. It turned out that André lost most but not all of his wealth. In the early 1930s, André sensed that the anti-Semitism taking root in Germany was more virulent than anything Jews had been exposed to in past. Not wanting to worry his family, he kept his concerns to himself, but he did take the precautionary measure of sending a small amount of gold and diamonds, a fraction of what he held, as a hedge against the unreliability of fiat currencies and financial institutions, to America for safekeeping. The amount was enough so the family didn't need to live like refugees when they arrived in America.

The Jewish community helped André rebuild the family business. It took some years, but eventually André was able to open another art-and-antiques gallery, first in Crown Heights; then by the 1970s, he relocated to the Upper East Side in Manhattan. His ancestors built the business from nothing and passed it down for future generations, and André was determined to rebuild the business so that he would also have something to pass down to his children and grandchildren. André tried not to get emotional about the loss of the art treasures, but the loss devastated him. His ancestors had entrusted him to safeguard the treasures for future generations, and he had failed.

What really weighed on André's conscience was the fact that his parents, siblings, aunts, uncles, and cousins, totaling sixty-eight relatives, had all decided to remain in France rather than flee. Throughout history, Jews were accustomed to anti-Semitism in Europe; it was fairly commonplace. His family mistakenly thought everything would be okay. By the time they realized they made a fatal miscalculation, it was too late. Every last one of them perished in the Nazi death camps. The survivor's guilt weighed heavily on the conscience of Nathalie's grandfather. The Holocaust erased his family's bloodline in Europe forever. Though André avoided the fate of those who were sent to the Nazi death camps, a part of him died nonetheless.

André could not undo what the Nazis had done to his family, but what he could do was to track down and recover each and every piece of art treasure and other valuables that the Nazis had stolen from him. The process of recovering the works proved to be frustratingly slow, but he found the work to be therapeutic. He hired a private investigator who had previously worked in the art unit at Interpol. André was able to find some of his family's artworks all around the world. Some were found listed in the catalogs of auction houses, others were displayed in museums, and yet others were found in private

collections. Sometimes the pieces were returned to the family without remuneration, in other cases the pieces needed to be repur-
chased, and yet in others the issue of ownership needed to be settled
by mediators or the courts.

André was eventually able to recover fifty-nine pieces of the family's 322-piece art collection. All the recovered artworks were traced
back to one of the railroad cars that contained 157 pieces. Not one of
the pieces recovered was from the missing second railroad car, which
contained 165 pieces. He knew this because the Germans kept such
meticulous records. At some point after the war, the Israelis came
into possession of these records and shared them with the affected
Jewish population of Europe to help piece together their lives in all
sorts of ways after the war. On occasion, the Israeli government took
it upon itself to recover art and other items on behalf of the Jewish
victims of the Third Reich. The Israeli government proved very help-
ful to the Rosenfeld family over the years, and André always sup-
ported them in return when he could. It was a mutually beneficial
relationship.

André never gave up the hope of someday finding the artworks from that second railroad car. Over the years, every so often
a rumor about the second railroad car would emerge from behind
the Iron Curtain. The talk was that at the end of the war, the Soviet
Trophy Brigades had seized that second railroad car, loaded with the
Rosenfeld's artworks, and transported it to the Soviet Union, where
the entire collection was placed directly into storage. André tried
to reach out to the Soviet government via diplomatic channels and
other third parties, but all efforts were futile. During the Cold War,
the Soviet Union closed itself off to the West, which made getting
any information an almost impossible task, especially on matters as
sensitive as looted art treasures.

In 1973, at the age of seventy, André turned over the reins of the gallery to Nathalie's father, Claude. Claude ran the business side of the gallery, and André dedicated his time solely toward art-recovery efforts. As the years passed, tracking down the family's lost treasures became much less of a priority for the other family members. Andre's children, namely Claude's older brother and sister, who, even though they were part owners of the gallery, had chosen career paths away from the family business. As selfish as it sounded, they didn't want their lives to be defined by the war. They knew how emotionally draining the work had been on their father, and they simply didn't care to inherit the emotional baggage that came with the gallery.

André respected the wishes of his two older children. As for himself, he was doing exactly what he had to do. What his children didn't quite appreciate but was understood by his granddaughter Nathalie was that his lifelong pursuit of the family's lost treasures was not just his own way of undoing what the Nazis had done to his family but was also his self-imposed penance for having cheated the fate that waited for his family after getting passage to America.

9

AFTER WORLD WAR II, because of Adolf Hitler's seemingly irrational decision to invade the Soviet Union, Germany found itself occupied and divided. A divided postwar Germany perfectly laid the groundwork for the Cold War confrontation between the United States and Soviet Union.

America's national security priority became the containment of the global Soviet threat, both military and political. With their mutual aversion to communism, the Nazis predictably went from being America's enemy to being its most valuable ally in the Cold War against the communist Soviet Union.

Even before Hitler rose to power, Germans had a proven track record in the field of science and technology, with an exceptional reputation for developing innovative military weapons. The Nazis took this to a whole new level, committing a staggering amount of resources to finance the most extraordinary laboratories, workshops, and factories, enabling Nazi scientists to create the most technologically advanced next generation of military weapons imaginable, dubbed *Wunder-Waffen*, or Wonder Weapons:

- Jet fighter aircraft (Messerschmitt 262); all American aircraft were engined by propeller
- Jet bomber aircraft (Arado 234)
- Long-range bomber jet (Messerschmitt 264), with a range of seven thousand miles and was dubbed the American bomber because it could have reached the east coast of the United States (for some curious reason it never went on a single bombing mission)
- Rocket-powered fighter plane (Messerschmitt 163)
- Aircraft with vertical landing and takeoff capabilities, which we now know as a helicopter
- Jet-powered rocket (V-1 rocket), which was the forerunner of today's cruise missile
- Liquid-fuel powered rocket (V-2 rocket), which was forerunner of today's ballistic missile and decades later played a crucial role in NASA's efforts to send a rocket to space
- Stealth fighter and bomber aircraft (Horton Ho 229), to which America's stealth aircraft of today looks remarkably similar
- Sturmgewehr 44, or STG 44, which is considered the world's first assault weapon
- Panzerschreck antitank portable bazooka, which is similar to today's rocket-propelled grenade (RPG)
- Night-vision technology
- Armor-plated tanks (Panzer) with stabilized guns for shooting while moving
- Fritz-X was a radio-guided glide bomb with seven hundred pounds of explosives

And there were countless others, some of which included technologies that defied linear science and were immediately "classified" by the US government at the end of the war and were never heard about again.

The US government and military were mesmerized by these awe-inspiring weapons, and they were willing to do whatever was necessary to get their hands on not only these weapons and technologies but also the Nazis behind them. These much sought-after Nazis came from a myriad of backgrounds: scientists, engineers, architects, technicians, doctors, industrialists, spy masters, and military personnel, among others.

The US government's plan was to recruit and resettle thousands of these Nazis in the United States, where they would work on the American side with the US government and military and in corporate America. The problem was, most of those being sought by the US government were considered war criminals and under normal circumstances would have been prevented from entering the United States. However, because their recruitment was deemed a national-security matter, ways were found around this.

The Office of Strategic Services (OSS), forerunner of the Central Intelligence Agency (CIA), was tasked with resettling these Nazis in America. The OSS was the nation's first intelligence agency and was established in the aftermath of the intelligence failure that resulted in the bombing of Pearl Harbor on December 7, 1941. The OSS recruited from Ivy League schools and filled its ranks with America's elite, who were also attached at the hip with Britain's aristocracy. The running joke about the OSS was that it stood for "Oh So Social" because the names of the agency's recruits read like America's social register: Dupont, Vanderbilt, Roosevelt, Morgan, Mellon, and so forth. Winston Churchill (whose mother was American) even had a cousin in the OSS.

It was no coincidence that the OSS recruits came from the same families of the industrialists and bankers who had greatly profited from their business relationships with the Nazis before and during the war. Now they were the same ones responsible for resettling their Nazi friends to America after the war. It was going to be through the OSS/CIA that America's shadow government would see to it that its agenda became America's agenda. "There is a shadow government running parallel to the US government that has no allegiance to the people," President John F. Kennedy said, who was the first Catholic president of the United States.

For the most-wanted Nazis, the OSS created new identities. The operation was named Operation Paperclip because the new sanitized identities and biographies were attached to their original file folders using a paperclip. Many Nazis were brought over in this manner and lived undetected in the States. It proved to be a highly valued operation in that it was able to, as effectively as possible, get German technology, both military and industrial, out of Germany at the end of the war while also keeping it out of the hands of the Soviets. As controversial as the program was, it was considered vital to America's national security.

Ultimately Operation Paperclip was responsible for resettling thousands of Nazis to America. Most of those who were relocated to the United States weren't just regular card-carrying members of the Nazi party but were the feverishly loyal and hardcore SS officers, all of whom had sworn an oath of loyalty to Hitler and the Nazi cause until death. The US government, in its haste and eagerness to acquire the Nazi wonder-weapons, and in an effort to keep those same weapons and technologies out of the hands of the Soviets, overlooked the threat posed by bringing so many Nazis and SS to the States.

In addition to the efforts of the OSS, there was another organization named ODESSA, which served a similar purpose. ODESSA, the Organization of Former SS Members, was created by the head of the SS, Heinrich Himmler. It is purported that ODESSA was only created at the end of the war when it became apparent that the Third Reich was going to be defeated; however, it's likely that ODESSA was always the plan. ODESSA served as a world-wide underground escape network that helped SS officers fleeing Germany after the war to secure false identity documents and passports from both the Vatican and the International Red Cross. These new identity papers and travel documents allowed thousands of SS officers to flee to Argentina, Chile, Brazil, Australia, Canada, Italy, Ireland, Portugal, Spain, Sweden, Switzerland, South Africa, Turkey, and throughout the African continent and the Middle East.

The OSS and ODESSA made it possible for these SS officers to not only escape prosecution for war crimes but also allowed them to conveniently transition into very strategic positions abroad. These SS officers, with their wealth of knowledge and expertise, were welcomed to the United States and around the world with open arms because in defeat they were no longer viewed as a threat. This was exactly what Adolf Hitler wanted the Americans and the world to believe. "Deceive the heavens to cross the ocean," as the ancient Chinese military stratagem suggests.

10

NATHALIE ROSENFELD WAS American by birth and held dual citizenship with France. English was her native language, though she spoke the most beautiful Parisian-accented French, which she learned from her grandfather. She was the envy of her brothers and cousins, none of whom spoke French as fluently as she did. When she and her grandfather spoke, it was always in French. André never wanted to return to Paris, the place where his family was betrayed by French collaborators, but it was still soothing to his ears to listen to Nathalie speaking his mother tongue. Nathalie was more like him than any of his children or grandchildren. She often sat for hours listening to him reminisce about life in Paris before his world came crashing down. She understood him in a way nobody else did. Nathalie was his favorite.

Nathalie attended Columbia University in Manhattan, where she earned both bachelor's and master's degrees in art history. Upon graduation in 1994, just three years after the passing of André, it came as no surprise to anyone in the family that she joined her father, Claude, at the family's art-and-antiques gallery on the Upper East Side. Before André passed, he tried to no avail to talk Nathalie out of continuing with his work at the gallery. For André, the work was his self-imposed penance, but it didn't need to be that way for Nathalie.

It wasn't her burden to inherit. She was free to do what the rest of the family did, which was move forward with their own lives and not allow the past to consume the present, as it did for André.

André naively wanted Nathalie to just find a nice man who came from a good Jewish family, get married, and have children of her own. As quaint as that plan was, it wasn't the path for Nathalie. Nathalie always knew that she would follow in her grandfather's footsteps and dedicated her life to recovering what the Nazis had stolen from him. This became her mission in life. As much as André didn't want that life for Nathalie, it brought him a degree of peace knowing that she would continue with recovery efforts where he left off.

Nathalie's work at the gallery started as a passion but quickly descended into an obsession. She was bold and fearless, with the unwavering resolve of an activist without any appreciation for the dangers involved. This proved to be her liability. She often found herself opposite many wealthy and powerful people who had come into possession of some of the looted art that rightfully belonged to her family. As far as she was concerned, she held the moral high ground for what she considered a righteous cause. She had a gift of being able to put people on the defensive and took pride in making powerful people squirm. Most wanted to conveniently forget that chapter in history, but not Nathalie. The way Nathalie saw it, she wanted all Nazis and anyone who profited from them to be held accountable, regardless of how much time had passed. *It was a matter of principle*, she thought.

She could be so sanctimonious at times. There was little else that infuriated Nathalie more than fellow Jews who owned German-made automobiles. In her mind, she could never reconcile, given what the Germans had done to Jews with the Holocaust, how any Jewish person could drive around in a German automobile. In her mind, this defied reason. Some defended themselves by saying that it was a matter of buying the best quality vehicles available, but for Nathalie, that point was inconsequential. *There was a principle involved*, she thought. Both of her older brothers owned German-made cars, and they refused to allow their sister, whom they considered irrationally rabid on this point, to bully them out of driving the vehicles they preferred. Her father, on the other hand, as much as he wanted a Mercedes sedan, settled on a Cadillac. He knew he wouldn't be able to standup to the withering criticism he would face from his own daughter. Claude loved his daughter dearly, but she had become so difficult to reason with on the subject.

Nathalie's work at the gallery earned her a place on the CIA's watch list, which wasn't a surprise given her extensive international travel; nonstop international calling; filing of countless lawsuits against governments, museums, and individuals; dealing with some unsavory characters in the art world; putting some prominent people on notice; communicating with foreign intelligence services, in particular the Israeli Mossad; and poking around on matters that most governments, including her own, just wanted to be forgotten. Because of the OSS/CIA's extensive and secret dealings with the Nazis, in pre- and postwar years, it was of the utmost importance for them to keep tabs on what Nathalie was working on. As a result, all of her communications and activities were monitored and analyzed, such as telephone calls, e-mails, faxes, Internet searches and history, travel, credit card spending, and any other information that could be collected.

Nathalie's relations with her family were strained, but for the most part, her self-righteousness was tolerated for several reasons. For Nathalie, it was never about the money; it was always a matter of principle. Even though only Nathalie and her father worked at the gallery, the others remained part owners. Whatever artworks Nathalie was able to recover, she unselfishly put back into the business for the benefit of the entire family. The others also took solace in the fact that Nathalie was spearheading the recovery efforts, which meant the burden was lifted from their shoulders. Secondly, she was such a good aunt to her nieces and nephews. Beyond buying the children thoughtful gifts for birthdays and holidays, she always made time for them. Nathalie was the one who took them to the movies, theater, and ice-skating rink—all the things children love. She was their only aunt, and the children loved her dearly. Nathalie had a maternal side, and if circumstances had been different, she easily could have had a family of her own. But for this life, that wasn't the path that was written for her.

When Nathalie went to work at the gallery, it had been almost three years since the collapse of the Soviet Union on December 26, 1991. Nathalie thought that the changing political landscape in Russia provided an opportunity to reach out to the Russian government once again, to try to learn the fate of the artworks from that second railroad car. The Russian's response was the same as it had always been; they claimed to know nothing whatsoever about her family's missing artwork.

It was like chasing a ghost, but Nathalie just wouldn't relent. In the spring of 1995, she traveled to Saint Petersburg, Russia, to view an exhibit at the world-renowned State Hermitage Museum titled *Hidden Treasures Revealed*. This exhibit marked the first time Russia had put on display any of the "trophy art" the Trophy Brigades had seized at the end of World War II. Nathalie attended the exhibit thinking that perhaps she could find a lead or make a contact that could help her but unfortunately, she came up empty-handed.

Nathalie's father and brothers were concerned about her safety. They often cautioned her against taking things too far, but she would hear none of it. Her intransigence made it difficult for anyone to talk any sense into her. Even a respected family friend who worked with Israeli intelligence at the Israeli Consulate in Manhattan had tried without success to persuade her to scale back her efforts. Given all the secrets that emerged from World War II, especially with regard to the looting that took place, it was only a matter of time before Nathalie, with her relentless determination, stumbled upon something that was never supposed to be discovered.

11

AFTER WORLD WAR II there was no time for America to savor its victory against the Third Reich; that would be left in the hands of Hollywood. A divided postwar Germany meant that the United States would go directly from World War II into the Cold War against its arch nemesis, the communist Soviet Union.

As far as the US government was concerned, the thousands of newfound Nazi friends who were resettled into America after the war couldn't have arrived at a more opportune time. Those who possessed knowledge and expertise of the Soviet Union were highly sought after by the military, CIA, FBI, and virtually every government agency. Once inside, these Nazis impressed senior American military and government officials with their vast knowledge of America's Cold War adversary. "Infiltrate your target. Initially, pretend to be a guest to be accepted, but develop from inside and become the owner later," an ancient Chinese military stratagem says.

The remaining Nazis would conveniently and seamlessly start their new lives working in corporate America to the benefit of America's capitalist elite. Not surprisingly, given their track record for developing the Hitler's awe-inspiring next-generation military weapons, many Nazis found themselves in positions throughout America's defense industry.

The SS intelligence officers who came to America were actively recruited by the CIA and military. These intelligence officers were highly coveted because they still had access to their extensive Nazi spy networks in place throughout the Soviet government, intelligence agencies, and military. These SS officers were quickly able to prove their value by providing American officials with a trove of classified Soviet intelligence reports, which confirmed America's worst fears: the Soviets had a unilateral, across-the-board military advantage against the United States in terms of the numbers and capabilities of nuclear missiles, methods to deliver these nuclear warheads, troops, tanks, fighter jets, and so on.

It would be learned decades later that the Soviet intelligence reports being supplied by the SS to the CIA and military were completely false. It had been the United States with the military advantage, not the Soviet Union. In hindsight, these Nazis worked in tandem with one another to spread misinformation at every turn throughout the US government and military.

Anyhow, at the time, the CIA and military then conveniently leaked these flawed reports to the corporate-owned lackey media, which then reported to the American people about the Soviet "missile gap" and other advantages against the United States. It's important to note that during this same period, SS intelligence officers were also providing the FBI with the names of Americans, purportedly obtained from their Soviet spy networks, who were communist sympathizers and spies. This opened an ugly chapter in American history from 1950 to 1954, known as the Red Scare or McCarthyism. This witch hunt for communists from within was eerily reminiscent of Hitler's incitement of communist fears in Germany following the Reichstag Fire.

Just as it did in Germany after the Reichstag Fire, the reports of the Soviet military advantage along with communist spies within instilled fear across the American public that there was a communist hiding under every bed. With all the hysteria circulating, the military, CIA, and FBI then demanded a massive spending increase, making it impossible for the president and Congress not to approve. This Cold War standoff proved to be an enduring conflict that lasted nearly fifty years, during which the American public was manipulated into a constant state of fear such that it was willing to make whatever sacrifices to support its government to address the communist threats at home and abroad. "There is no instance of a nation benefitting from prolonged warfare," said Sun Tzu, in *The Art of War.*

Before World War II there had never been a dedicated defense sector in the United States. In the past, the government was able to commandeer any manufacturer for wartime production of armaments or whatever was needed to support the war effort. After the war the manufacturer would switch back to its normal business operations. The same went for the military. Before World War II the United States didn't have a standing army. One would be assembled to fight in whatever given conflict; then after it was over, the army would be disbanded. The Cold War changed these paradigms forever. The United States was gearing up for a constant state of war with the Soviet Union, which demanded a staggering level of commitment and financial resources. America's elite and corporate America stood to benefit immensely from this out-of-control defense spending at the expense of America.

This unrestrained defense spending led to the "military-industrial complex," which is the relationship between the military and defense industries who, with their combined ability, can push their own agenda and influence public opinion. To further blur the lines of conflict of interest, many high-level military officials retire and then take jobs with defense contractors, who then exploit their military relation-ships for the benefit of their new employers. The defense industries also directly influence the White House and Congress through politi-cal contributions as a means to lobby for increased military spending or for specific projects.

This unsustainable level of military spending is precisely what President Eisenhower warned against in his farewell speech in January 1961, when he said, "We must guard against the acquisition of unwar-ranted influence, whether sought or unsought, by the military-industrial complex. The potential for the disastrous rise of misplaced power exists and will persist." President Eisenhower was a retired five-star general who during World War II served as the supreme commander of the Allied Forces in Europe.

It was that easy for the Nazis to hijack America's agenda. Regardless of whether the CIA and military knew they were being manipulated by the Nazis, it didn't matter because they also stood to benefit financially from the massive increase in government spend-ing. The same went for America's elite. Just as they reaped massive profits by helping the Third Reich prepare for war against Europe and the United States, they were now poised to garner unfathomable profits from America's Cold War with the Soviet Union.

To this day, long after the Cold War has ended, America's defense sector continues to grow at an unsustainable rate. The United States spends more on defense than the next twenty countries combined. America's astronomical level of debt is pushing the country to the brink of financial ruin. Ultimately America's staggering level of debt, not some external threat, will prove to be our nation's greatest national security threat. "The supreme art of war is to subdue the enemy without fighting," Sun Tzu said, in *The Art of War.*

12

THE MAN AT the restaurant who passed the envelope to Nathalie was indeed Russian. His name was Vasili Borisovich, and he had worked at the Kremlin Archives in Moscow for the past thirty-five years. The Kremlin Archives are the central repository for the government's most closely guarded secrets. Given Vasili's graduate degree in art history, he was assigned to the art unit. In his position, he had access to information relating to the "trophy art" seized by the Soviet Army Trophy Brigades at the end of World War II.

The last fifteen years had taken a devastating toll on Vasili's frame of mind. His life began to unravel in January 1985, five years after the Soviet military, in an attempt to counter a growing Islamic insurgency on its border, invaded Afghanistan. The younger of his two sons was drafted into the Soviet Army and deployed to Afghanistan. Thirteen weeks after his son arriving in-country, Vasili was notified by the Ministry of Defense that his son had been killed in action. The official version of events was that he was killed when his platoon, while on patrol in eastern Afghanistan, was ambushed by the Afghan mujahideen (holy warriors). As it would be for any parent, the news was devastating.

With Soviet casualties mounting, it became apparent that Afghanistan had turned into the Soviet Union's Vietnam. After ten years of fighting and nearly fifteen thousand Soviet soldiers killed, the Soviet military eventually withdrew from Afghanistan in defeat in 1989. As was the case with Alexander the Great, Genghis Khan, various Persian empires (Iran), India, and Great Britain, the Soviets also learned firsthand why Afghanistan was known as "The Graveyard of Empires."

The Soviet's defeat in Afghanistan was an omen for things to come. Later that same year, the facade of communism began to crumble with the fall of the Berlin Wall on November 9, 1989. This set in motion a chain of events that two years later culminated in the breakup of the Soviet Union on Christmas Day in 1991. Vasili, along with the rest of the population, had been entirely disillusioned by the farce of Soviet-styled communism, which they had taken hook, line, and sinker.

After the breakup of the Soviet Union, Russia became one of fifteen stand-alone republics. Democratic and capitalist reforms were put on the fast track. Russian words such as *glasnost* and *perestroika*, meaning "openness" and "restructuring" respectively, became part of the everyday lexicon, not just in Russia but around the world. For a short time, there was good reason to be hopeful.

The top priority of the Russian government was to transition the centrally planned economy, which under the communist system had been managed by bureaucrats in Moscow, to a capitalist free-market model in which prices for goods and services are determined, free from government control, by market forces such as supply and demand. For this transition to happen, two things needed to be done. First, state-owned industries and assets, which included everything from land and retail stores to oil companies, had to be privatized. This essentially meant selling off these assets into private ownership. Second, government regulated price-controls had to be removed in order to allow market forces to determine the costs of goods and services.

This privatization of government assets proved to be nothing more than a power play by government insiders. These insiders, with their political connections, were able to hijack the privatization process and deliver the massive state industries to themselves, thus reaping hundreds of billions of dollars in profits. Those insiders are today's Russia's billionaire oligarchs.

An unintended consequence of dumping all these government assets onto the open market at the same time was that the Russian economy received a massive infusion of capital all at once, while at the same time, the government had removed price-controls for everyday goods. This caused inflation to skyrocket, which for Vasili and the average Russian meant that virtually overnight salaries, pensions, and savings had become worthless. Vasili had committed his life to Soviet-modeled communism, and now he'd lost everything and had no fallback plan.

In January 1995, Vasili left Moscow and took a temporary one-year assignment in Saint Petersburg, where he helped the Ministry of Culture organize an art exhibit titled *Hidden Treasures Revealed*. The exhibit was at the world-renowned State Hermitage Museum and was held from March 29 to October 29, 1995. The exhibition put on display about one hundred paintings from the massive trove of trophy art that the Soviet Army had taken from Germany at the end of World War II. Given Russia's silence for so long on the matter of looted art treasures, the exhibit was considered a major breakthrough across the art world. Vasili's assignment was to assist in identifying the least controversial pieces for display. These works included paintings by artists such as Degas, Vincent van Gogh, Renoir, Matisse, Monet, and others. Visitors traveled from around the world to take a glimpse at works of art that had been hidden from the world for close to fifty years.

It was in the spring of 1999 when Vasili was back at the Kremlin Archives in Moscow that a letter crossed his desk. The letter had been received by the Ministry of Foreign Affairs from Nathalie Rosenfeld. She was searching for her family's lost artworks from that second railroad car. Vasili received a copy of the correspondence for informational purposes, but it was the ministry that was preparing its standard response to these types of inquiries. Before the breakup of the Soviet Union, Vasili would have never received a copy of Nathalie's letter, but in this new era, the art unit was kept somewhat abreast of relevant matters. Vasili knew the story behind the Rosenfeld collection and even knew precisely where it was kept in storage. He also knew that the artworks, totaling 165 pieces, had remained intact and in good condition.

Nathalie's letter planted the seed of betrayal with Vasili. He knew the information to which he had access was worth at least a few million dollars to the right people. Rather than taking on the risk involved with shopping around these secrets, it occurred to him to make a targeted approach to Nathalie, a fellow Jew, whose family in his opinion were still the rightful owners of the artworks. Given his much-compromised frame of mind, Vasili had no qualms justifying his plan. Vasili was certain that the Rosenfeld woman would easily be willing to pay one to two million dollars for proof that his government was in possession of the artworks. This seemed like the most expedient way to solve his pension issue.

Vasili dared not contact Nathalie while in Russia. He knew very well that, despite the much-hyped democratic reforms in Russia, it was still very much an authoritarian police state, with the government monitoring all communications, domestic and international. Vasili arranged with the Ministry of Culture to be added to an official delegation that was traveling to New York later that year in December. The delegation was to deliver twelve paintings that the State Hermitage Museum was loaning to the Metropolitan Museum of Art in Manhattan. It was on this trip that Vasili intended to make contact with Nathalie, without fear of his communications being monitored. That was his plan, and it seemed simple enough, or so he thought.

13

ON WHAT WAS supposed to be an ordinary Monday morning, two days before the as-of-yet unscheduled rendezvous at Au Bon Pain, a man with a Russian accent called the Rosenfeld Art and Antiques Gallery, which was located on Madison Avenue between Seventy-Ninth and Eightieth Streets.

"Good morning, Rosenfeld Art and Antiques," answered the receptionist.

"Good morning, can I speak with a Ms. Nathalie Rosenfeld?" asked the unknown caller.

"Whom might I ask is calling?"

"Ms. Rosenfeld doesn't know me, but my name is Vasili."

"Please hold a moment while I check to see if she's in the office." The receptionist already knew that Nathalie was in the office but wanted to give her the option of whether or not to accept the call from the caller with a Russian accent.

It was a warm transfer. "Nathalie, I have a man on the telephone who has a thick Russian accent. His name is Vasili. He said you didn't know him." Nathalie was intrigued. *It could be an interesting way to start the week*, she thought.

"That's okay, you can put him through," responded Nathalie.

"Hello, this is Nathalie Rosenfeld; how can I help you?"

"Hello, my name is Vasili, and I'm the one who can help you."

"What makes you think I need your help?" responded Nathalie.

"You need my help if you want back your family's artworks from that second railroad car you and your grandfather have been searching for. Your suspicions are correct; my government has been in possession of your family's collection since the end of the war, fifty-four years ago."

Nathalie was trying her best to remain calm, but her heart started pounding, and for a brief moment, the air in her lungs simply disappeared, and she gasped for air. He had her undivided attention. She quickly composed herself and was trying to be coy, but the fact was she was hanging on his every word. She was accustomed to being the one to put others on edge, but now she was the one thrown off balance. The art world is filled with unscrupulous characters, always trying to pull off some type of fraud or con, but something about this caller seemed genuine.

Not wanting to be tricked into revealing anything herself, she put the ball back in his court and asked, "I don't know what second railroad car you're talking about."

"Ms. Rosenfeld, I saw the recent letter that you sent the Russian Ministry of Foreign Affairs asking for information regarding the artworks that belong to your family from that second railroad car."

While remaining seated at her desk and holding the telephone to her left ear, Nathalie swiveled her chair, allowing her right arm to extend to the bottom drawer of the filing cabinet to the right of her desk. She opened the drawer and removed a tattered manila file folder that contained a catalog of each piece of art and antiques that had been confiscated from her grandfather. The photocopied documents were Wehrmacht documents, written in German by the Kunstschutz unit that had seized her grandfather's artworks. The documents meticulously listed each of the 322 items confiscated. This was such a critical document in that it documented, with German bureaucratic thoroughness, the contents of both railroad cars. The document had been obtained in the postwar years by the Israelis, who then provided André with a copy. Nathalie already knew the contents of that railroad car by heart but felt it necessary to keep the document in front of her while she quizzed the stranger on the phone.

"Vasili, can you please tell me the contents of that second railroad car?"

"I can do better. I have pictures," stated Vasili.

"Vasili, you need to convince me that you know the contents before we go any further," stated Nathalie, in a firm tone.

He rattled off the names of twelve paintings on the list before she stopped him. She sat in silence in her chair, with her mouth partially agape. The moment was surreal.

"How many pieces remain from that railroad car, Vasili?" asked Nathalie.

"There are one hundred sixty-five items in total. The entire collection went directly into storage and is locked away. When the army returned home with millions upon millions of items, at a time when nearly five hundred museums had been looted and destroyed by the Nazis, the only thing we could do was put everything into storage. Consider yourself lucky by the way; many of the artworks that survived the war ended up being destroyed by terrible storage conditions."

Nathalie was almost speechless at this point. For all these years, her grandfather had been searching for the contents from this second railroad car, and now it seemed that she might be able to get half the collection back in one deal. It seemed too good to be true. She then took an ambivalent tone.

"Why are you contacting me and not someone else?" asked Nathalie.

"It's too risky for me to shop around this sort of information. The art world is small, and I'd be discovered. Besides, I had access to information that I knew was of great value to you. Your letter to the Ministry of Foreign Affairs is what gave me the idea to contact you, a fellow Jew. I'm in Manhattan now. I traveled all this way to speak only to you."

Nathalie could sense the sincerity in Vasili's voice, but she was never the trusting type. She just could never allow herself to trust someone on a leap of faith. That wasn't her style. The fact of the matter was, Vasili was a stranger she knew nothing about.

"If you have the proof you claim to have, I would be willing to pay, but we're not discussing any of those details until I see this supposed evidence you claim to have. I want to see a sampling of the photographs. I don't even want to have another conversation until I've had the opportunity to review and authenticate the pictures," she stated with authority.

"I'm staying at the Marriott Hotel in Times Square. We can meet at the cafe downstairs," stated Vasili.

"No, I'm not going there. We will meet at a restaurant called Au Bon Pain. It's less than a block away from Times Square on Forty-Eighth Street between the Fifth Avenue and the Avenue of the Americas. We can meet two days from now, on Wednesday at one o'clock p.m.," said Nathalie. She chose this location because she knew that the restaurant would be packed with many witnesses in case something went wrong.

"I don't know what you look like. How will I find you at the restaurant?" he asked.

"You'll know when you see me," Nathalie said, with confidence.

14

MIDWAY THROUGH WORLD War II, the US Army's Signal Intelligence Service (SIS), forerunner of the National Security Agency (NSA), partnered with Great Britain's codebreaking and eavesdropping services. By this time the British had already broken the code for the Nazi Enigma machines, which were sophisticated cipher machines that encrypted secret Nazi communications. Essentially what this meant was that Great Britain was able to read the Third Reich's secret communications.

Because the Nazi secret codes were already broken, the SIS and Great Britain jointly launched the Venona Project. This project was responsible for the interception, decryption, and analysis of messages sent by the Soviet diplomatic, military, and intelligence services. Despite the Soviets being allies in the fight against the Nazis, the Americans and British still closely monitored their every communication.

After the war the United States and Great Britain solidified their cooperation on the sharing of signals intelligence (conversations and electronic signals) and entered into the UKUSA Agreement of 1948.

However, the UKUSA Agreement of 1948 surreptitiously took on a life of its own, evolving into the world's largest top-secret data collection operation, known as the Echelon Program. The Echelon Program, though not formally established until 1971, consists of the code-breaking and eavesdropping agencies of its five core members: USA (NSA), UK (GCHQ), Canada (CSEC), Australia (DSD), and New Zealand (GCSB). Collectively, this group is also known as the "Five Eyes" because it knows everything happening around the globe at all times.

America's newfound Nazi friends, who, under the Third Reich, had built an amazingly technologically advanced surveillance apparatus, were the ones who played an intricate role in designing and building the technological web of the Echelon Program. The surveillance infrastructure consisted of a vast array of Earth-orbiting satellites, land-based satellite dishes, and radio towers located around the globe and had the ability to tap into the extensive network of undersea communication cables along with other means. Hand-carried notes were about the only communications that were able to evade this signals-intelligence dragnet.

The Echelon Program was not designed to target the communications of specific individuals but rather to vacuum up and store all the signals intelligence of the entire world, including those of its own citizens. Each member of the Five Eyes is able to bypass its own government's privacy and warrantless search laws simply by not intercepting the communications of its own citizens but having a partner agency do it. For instance, the UK (GCHQ) would be responsible for the interception and storage of the communications of US citizens. However, the NSA then has complete warrantless access to the GCHQ databases. This arrangement allows the NSA to say that it doesn't conduct electronic surveillance of its own citizens without a warrant, which is technically true, but not true in terms of the spirit of America's laws governing privacy rights and warrantless searches.

The Echelon Program intercepts and stores all encrypted and unencrypted communications, such as telephone, fax, radio, radar, and e-mails. As technologies have advanced, so hasn't the program. When the Internet became more accessible to the public in the 1980s, everything the user does on the Internet can be collected and analyzed as well, such as social-media activity, browsing history, credit-card purchases, spending habits, geolocation information, gas station fill-ups, bank records, travel itineraries, and medical records. Today we call this data mining, but it has been going on since the 1950s.

The data was then routed to the algorithm-driven supercomputers at NSA headquarters in Fort Meade, Maryland, or at the overseas storage facilities of the partners. The complex algorithms then index the data based on telephone numbers, fax numbers, e-mail addresses, IP addresses, social security numbers, keywords, and so forth. Once the data is indexed, it then becomes searchable by those with access to the databases.

These algorithm-driven computers merely extract whatever information the algorithms tell them to extract. This data then needs to be reviewed by an intelligence analyst to determine if anything is significant. When the technology exists, if it doesn't already, these algorithm-driven systems will be replaced by artificial intelligence (AI) systems. These AI systems will be able to replace the human element, which will allow the systems to more efficiently analyze the data collected and draw its own conclusions.

AI will be able to aggregate a whole myriad of data points for each individual, which will then be used to determine a person's personality and psychological profile. Prediction algorithms are already being used to process these data points in order to determine or anticipate a people's behavior. With that information, these government entities know precisely how to manipulate, brainwash, and control the population. This surveillance apparatus is far beyond what the Nazis ever had in place. This data being collected is knowledge, and knowledge is power. And power is always abused—always, always.

15

VASILI'S PLAN WAS doomed from the moment he telephoned Nathalie. Nathalie's killing had nothing to do with the pictures that the Russian was trying to sell her. Her fate had been sealed two weeks prior to Vasili's telephone call. Nathalie was killed because, while following the trail of the gold and diamonds that were also stolen from her grandfather by the Nazis, under mysterious circumstances she came into possession of a highly secret list of the names and account numbers of Adolf Hitler's most loyal SS officers who fled Germany after the war.

Nathalie didn't know the significance of the list but suspected something nefarious. There was only one person she dared mention the list to, and he was a family friend named Yonatan. Yonatan was a diplomatic attaché at the Israeli Consulate in Manhattan. Nathalie had always suspected he worked for the Mossad, which was Israeli's equivalent of the CIA, but he never shared that with her. Yonatan immediately recognized the names on the list but didn't betray that fact. He also recognized the eighteen-digit alphanumeric account numbers as World War II-era accounts from Switzerland.

Yonatan knew having this list was equivalent to a death sentence for Nathalie. He asked her how she came into possession of the list, but she refused to provide any details. Yonatan had worked with Nathalie on a number of occasions to help recover her family's art-works, and he knew how obstinate she could be. For her own safety, he wanted her to turn over the list, but she flat out refused. She did, however, allow him to make a copy. He cautioned her against follow-ing up on the list in the strongest of terms, but she refused to com-mit. Nathalie's problem was that she didn't scare easily, if at all. She never knew when to back off.

Nathalie's fatal mistake was that she naively typed some of the names and account numbers into an Internet search engine to try to learn anything about the origin of the accounts. What Nathalie didn't realize was that the National Security Agency (NSA), America's code-breaking and eavesdropping organization, monitored everything on the Internet. The account numbers that Nathalie obtained, along with tens of millions of other specific search terms, were actively sought by algorithm-driven supercomputers at the NSA. Anytime one of the flagged items was searched on the Internet, or written in an e-mail or spoken over the telephone, the NSA would be notified. The NSA was that good.

When Nathalie performed an Internet search of some of the names and account numbers, the NSA alerted the CIA that names and accounts the agency had flagged had been searched for online by someone already on its watch list. The notification was then routed to a group that doesn't even officially exist. Those who know refer to this group as the CIA within the CIA, or the Shadow CIA. It was this shadow group at the CIA that handled all matters concerning Nazis to ensure that nobody, other than the deepest inner sanctum of America's shadow government, ever knows the truth about the OSS's secret relationship with Adolf Hitler and the Nazis.

Unbeknown to Nathalie, the list of names and accounts were part of the Black Eagle Trust. This trust, named in deference to the Nazis, had been established by a shadow element within the OSS, whose allegiance was not to America but rather to a worldwide shadow government. This trust was being used to transfer funds to Adolf Hitler's most loyal SS officers who had relocated to the United States and around the globe at the end of the war. These names and accounts threatened to expose the Nazi conspirators behind Adolf Hitler's secret plot against America.

Nathalie Rosenfeld's fate was sealed the instant it was learned that she was in possession of these account numbers. This was why Nathalie had to be killed, but the group wanted to avoid being directly involved in the killing of an American on US soil. As far as the CIA was concerned, Vasili couldn't have contacted Nathalie at a more opportune time. The CIA seized the opportunity to enlist Russian intelligence (SVR) under the guise of allowing the Russians to handle their own traitor, on the condition that they kill Nathalie. The CIA deliberately decided not to reveal the identity of the traitor, Vasili Borisovich, because they didn't want the SVR to head off the exchange without taking care of Nathalie. The CIA tabled the matter in a way as to make it look as though they were doing the Russians a favor by allowing them to handle their own turncoat and to eliminate the woman who intended to use the pictures to blackmail the Russian government into returning her family's artworks. Russians hate being blackmailed.

The CIA gave the Russians just one condition: Nathalie had to be killed discreetly, which meant no witnesses and no blood. Her death had to look like she died of natural causes so that nobody would even suspect that she had been murdered. The Russians have extensive experience killing quietly. The CIA liked the plan, as it allowed them to use their enemy to do the agency's dirty work for them without the Russians ever knowing.

16

THE EIGHT-PERSON SVR team was already in place by the time Nathalie arrived at Au Bon Pain at 12:40 p.m. The primary surveillance vehicle was an unassuming white van with tinted windows, the same type used as delivery vehicles throughout the city. The van arrived early and circled the block several times before a space opened up on Forty-Eighth Street across from the restaurant, where it had the perfect view of people arriving and departing Au Bon Pain. Inside the van were two members of the team, one of whom was the team leader of the operation, named Victor Yurchenko, a hardened twenty-year veteran at the KGB/SVR. Victor joined the agency after completing his university degree in 1980. His first assignment was in Afghanistan and then in Lebanon and Chechnya, among others.

The second vehicle was a black 1995 Ford Explorer and was positioned half a block away on the corner of Forty-Eighth Street and Sixth Avenue, on the edge of Times Square. This vehicle contained three members of the team whose task was to take into custody the Russian traitor after he left the restaurant. The plan was that they would then take the traitor to a warehouse in a remote part of the Russian enclave of Brighton Beach in Brooklyn, where he would be interrogated, after which he'd most certainly meet an extrajudicial end.

Two other members of the team, a man and the only woman, were already inside the restaurant when Nathalie arrived. They sat at a table off to the right, pretending to eat lunch while taking turns looking at a tourist map. All the team members had a small radio wired along the inside of their left sleeve and an almost invisible earpiece, allowing them to communicate with one another. The couple was placed inside so they could provide the team outside with a description of the traitor and confirm when the pictures were passed to the woman. Most importantly, they would inform the others when the targets left the restaurant.

The eighth member of the team was the man with the ice-cold blue eyes. He was walking in the area and waiting to receive word when Nathalie was leaving the restaurant so he could time his movements accordingly. Because of the short notice for the operation, he only had one day to surveil her. Like most Manhattanites, who can't be bothered with a car, she traveled by taxi throughout the city. He surmised that she would leave the restaurant heading east, knowing that taking a taxi from that direction would be easiest for her to return to the family's gallery on the Upper East Side. Even if she went in the opposite direction, he had a contingency for that possibility as well. He was a professional, and professionals always have contingency plans.

Victor had been waiting in the van, behind tinted windows, with camera in hand. Field operatives learn to always be ready, eyes peeled and looking for anything out of the ordinary. He was the first to see Nathalie approach and reported her arrival over the radio. He matter-of-factly snapped a few pictures of her as she approached the restaurant. Victor didn't even take notice that she was perhaps the most beautiful woman who had crossed his path that day. As far as he was concerned, she was an enemy of the Russian government, nothing more. He had no reservations about what had to be done.

The couple inside the restaurant watched as Nathalie, having arrived early, patiently waited off to the side for a table to clear that had a direct line of sight with the entrance. When the patrons at one of the tables she was eying cleared, she sat and calmly waited. The Russian couple was positioned slightly behind her over her left shoulder, along the side wall.

As Victor waited for the unknown traitor to arrive, someone caught his attention. A man in his late twenties was approaching the restaurant. This man clearly wasn't the Russian he was waiting for, but there was something about him that compelled Victor to take the man's picture anyway.

The couple inside didn't even notice when the man in his late twenties entered the restaurant and got to the back of the long line to order. But they did notice when his undivided attention shifted to the same woman they were surveilling. They watched his brow furrow as he observed her. It looked as though he was trying to make sense of her presence. They didn't know what to make of it, so they radioed this development to Victor and provided him a description: brown wavy hair, blue eyes, milk-white skin, slightly under six feet, about 170 pounds, wearing a dark-blue overcoat, dark-blue suit and tie, and black shoes. Victor knew exactly who they were talking about.

Everything suddenly got more complicated when this un- known man in his late twenties noticed Nathalie's reaction when the distinct-looking Russian entered the restaurant. The couple radioed the description of the Russian as planned and continued watching. They clearly saw that this man witnessed the entire exchange. The couple radioed the others when the Russian and woman left the restaurant so the others could play their roles. It was when they were getting ready to stand that they saw the witness awkwardly, obviously unplanned, get out of line to pursue the woman. The couple quickly radioed to the others what was happening.

Victor managed to snap another picture of this unknown man on his way out of the restaurant, but there was nothing anyone could do. The man with the ice-cold blue eyes was already approaching Nathalie for the kill, and Victor made clear that the operation had to go forward regardless. They would deal with the witness later. The SVR team couldn't take any chance of Nathalie escaping the scene with the manila envelope.

The couple followed the witness out the door and saw that he witnessed the assassin bump into the woman; then a moment later she collapsed dead. He then watched as the trained killer removed the envelope from her handbag. There weren't supposed to be any witnesses, they knew. Victor instructed the couple to tail the witness after he left the scene. Victor already had a few pictures of the witness but wanted to know if there was anything else they could learn. They tried to follow but lost sight of him in Rockefeller Plaza among the throng of holiday tourists.

17

I EXITED THE elevator on the eleventh floor and then passed through the double glass doors to the right, which led to the offices of Lucent Technologies. As I hurried past the receptionist's desk, she must have sensed something wasn't right because she asked, "Is everything all right, David?"

Barely making eye contact, I replied, "Everything is fine, Carol." Without giving it a second thought, her attention returned to her tabloid newspaper.

Once through reception area, I passed through another set of double glass doors that led down a thirty-foot hallway, which opened up to an open-area about half the size of a basketball court. The space was filled with about seventy-five office cubicles. The dividers were about shoulder height when sitting, making it look like a room full of groundhogs peering out across the office prairie. This sight served as a daily reminder of my unrealized personal goals.

My cubicle was off to the far right of the room. I sat down at my desk and pretended to fidget with my laptop. But what I was actually doing was taking a series of slow, deep, breaths to calm my nerves and regain my composure so that I could process everything I saw and then figure out what to do.

As much as I tried to calm my nerves, the gravity of the situation bore down on me hard. I couldn't stop thinking about the mystery woman. One minute she was so alive, then just minutes later she's murdered right before my eyes. Yet despite being killed on a crowded sidewalk, nobody even saw anything except me. If I hadn't taken up pursuit, then the man wearing the fedora with the ice-cold blue eyes would have never been noticed. But the cost of being the lone witness to the woman's murder was that it was only me the killer stared down. How did he even know I was there? When I got out of line to follow the mystery woman, I had an eerie feeling that danger lurked. The handoff must have been under surveillance. Whoever was watching must have alerted the killer of my presence. That was all I could come up with at that point.

What possessed me to follow in the first place? I asked myself. The real question should have been more along the lines of how could I not have followed her. As incredibly beautiful as she was, it wasn't a sexual attraction that drew me to her; it was something else entirely. From the instant I noticed the woman, I couldn't take my eyes off her. She clearly didn't blend with the other patrons, but there was something else. It was almost as if there was something we shared, or a likeness of sorts.

My attention shifted back to the package that was handed to the mystery woman. The manila envelope wasn't full-sized but closer to six by nine. The envelope was about an inch thick, and it bulged to the edges. Whatever it was fit tightly inside. The envelope was too large for the contents to have been currency, not even if it were a stack of the much larger 500-euro notes. Regardless, I was certain that a woman with her presence and demeanor was not the type who would receive an envelope full of cash. Given the fact that she was killed for the envelope, something very sensitive must have been inside.

There was so much to process, it was making my head spin. I pushed my chair away from the desk, rested my elbows on my knees, and lowered my face into my open hands. What did I get myself into? One minute I'm having a typical uneventful day, then the next minute I witnessed a murder—but not just any murder. My intuition told me that something dark loomed behind the killing of this mystery woman.

I sat upright and leaned back in my chair, my fingers interlaced behind my head, and looked out across all the cubicles. *What a depressing sight*, I thought. My life's goals had taken a backseat to the realities of life. Since graduating college, my goal had been to work overseas in some third-world country with just the right amount of strife to keep things interesting. I didn't want to be an observer in life; I wanted to be involved. However, getting overseas proved to be more difficult than I had imagined. Whether applying for a position at the United Nations or the many international nonprofit humanitarian relief organizations, I was repeatedly told that without the relevant overseas experience, I wasn't eligible for the positions. It was a classic catch-22: without the experience I wasn't qualified for the job, but the only way I could get the experience was by getting a job.

Long story short, that's how I found myself in this sea of cubicles in corporate America. It felt as though I had sold my soul. I had become what I feared most—one of the minions, nothing more than a cog in the wheel. Where had I gone so wrong in my life to end up selling, of all things, voice messaging systems? Everyone hates when they get voice mail when they're trying to reach someone, and yet this is what I was wasting my life doing. I wanted so much more out of life, but nothing was working out.

There was nothing else to reconcile. I knew what had to be done. As the sole witness to her murder, I had to come forward and tell the police everything I saw. There was no way I could remain silent. My conscience would have never allowed it. If I didn't go to the police, it was likely they would never realize that the woman had been murdered. Despite sensing there was more than met the eye with what I had witnessed, for the second time in an hour, I threw caution to the wind.

Before heading back downstairs, I needed to ask my manager if she could cover my sales meeting that was scheduled to begin in about thirty minutes.

The sales meeting was scheduled on short notice, only about two weeks before the year 2000. The news media and everyone else for that matter were calling it the start of the new millennium, but if they had any sense, they would know that doesn't happen until 2001. For the past year, convinced it was merely a sales push, the client had stubbornly refused to upgrade his company's voice messaging systems to something that was Y2K compliant. The Y2K bug (a.k.a. millennium bug) concerns were rooted in the fact that computer programmers had always only used two digits to express the year rather than four. Those claiming to be computer experts theorized that when the calendar changed from December 31, 1999, to January 1, 2000, the computers would interpret the 00 date as being 1900, not 2000. This would then cause computers worldwide to crash. It was the constant media onslaught hyping apocalyptic scenarios and exploiting people's fears that eventually weakened my client's resolve to forego the upgrade.

I stood from my chair and walked toward one of the highly coveted perimeter offices with a window.

"Hello, Eileen, do you have a moment?"

"Sure, what is it?"

"While on my lunch break a little while ago, I saw a woman drop dead on the sidewalk, across the plaza near Au Bon Pain."

"How awful! What happened?"

"I'm not sure. I didn't think much of it, so I came back to the office, but in hindsight, I think I may have seen something that no one else saw. I should at least return to the scene and mention it to the police while they are down there."

"Sure, what do you need from me?"

"Can you cover my two o'clock meeting? It's with the client we discussed yesterday. Before I went to lunch, I set up everything in the conference room. It's our Y2K client presentation."

"Go talk to the police, and I'll take care of the presentation," said Eileen.

"Thanks so much, Eileen. I'll be back as soon as possible."

"Take as long as you need," said Eileen.

"Okay, thanks."

It was empowering to be returning to the scene on my own volition. For the first time in a long time, I knew I was doing precisely what I was meant to be doing. The mystery woman had commanded my complete and undivided attention in a way that didn't make sense. It was as if my noticing her had already been written. I was convinced that the feeling of being strangely pulled to follow her was not only for me to bear witness to her murder, but there seemed to be something beyond waiting to be discovered, or something like that.

18

BY THE TIME I returned to the spot where the mystery woman was killed, the first responders were long gone. There was nothing to indicate that only an hour earlier, a young beautiful woman had been murdered. It was obvious the police didn't realize this was a crime scene; otherwise the sidewalk would have been taped off for investigators. *Of course they didn't know it was a crime scene*, I thought. Nobody else saw the man with the ice-cold blue eyes except me.

With thoughtful deliberation, I removed my cell phone from my coat pocket and called 911.

"Nine one one, what is your emergency?" asked the operator.

"Hi, I don't have an emergency. I'm calling about the woman who died in the middle of the sidewalk on Forty-Eighth Street near Fifth Avenue less than an hour ago."

"What about her?" asked the operator.

"I'd like to speak to the police about something I saw before she collapsed."

"Please hold; I'm going to transfer you to that precinct."

After about five rings, someone answered the line. "Eighteenth Precinct."

Expecting him to ask how he can help, I waited, but there was nothing but dead air. After a short stutter, I said, "Hello, my name is David Walker. Can I speak to someone about the woman who died an hour ago on Forty-Eighth Street near Fifth Avenue?"

"What about?"

"I saw something suspicious before she collapsed."

"Can you come to the precinct to speak with a detective?"

"Sure; where are you located?"

"We're at Three-Oh-Six West Fifty-Fourth Street, between Eighth and Ninth Avenues," said the desk sergeant. "Your name is David Walker, right?"

"Yes, I'm walking now. I'll see you in about fifteen minutes."

After the desk sergeant hung up, he dialed the extension for Detective Lorenzo. "Detective, about forty-five minutes ago, a twenty-nine-year-old woman named Nathalie Rosenfeld collapsed dead on the sidewalk on Forty-Eighth between Fifth and Sixth Avenues. She was DOA at Mount Sinai; apparently she went into massive cardiac arrest. There weren't any signs of foul play. However, a witness just called, and he claims to have seen something suspicious before she collapsed."

"What's his name?" asked the detective.

"His name is David Walker, and he's on his way to the precinct to speak with you," replied the desk sergeant.

"Ring me when he arrives."

"Will do."

19

AFTER WORLD WAR II the OSS was disbanded, and its successor, the Central Intelligence Agency (CIA), was founded under the National Security Act of 1947. Though it would be a newly created spy agency, the shadow presence of America's elite in the OSS would continue forward at the CIA, where Hitler's most loyal SS officers would be brought into the fold. Together, America's shadow government and Hitler's SS would pursue an agenda that would come at the expense of America.

The CIA's charter stated that the agency would be responsible for intelligence and espionage activities outside of the United States. The charter explicitly prohibited the agency from carrying out operations on US soil. From the outset, President Truman had concerns that without proper oversight, the agency could take on a life of its own.

It's easy to be distracted by the impressive array of next-generation military technologies developed under the Third Reich, but the real power achieved by the Nazis, with carefully crafted propaganda, was their ability to manipulate and brainwash the entire German population. This feat was even more remarkable given that the German people were some of the most intellectual in the entire world during this time. The German people were at the intellectual forefront in nonlinear advanced science (i.e., quantum physics), psychology, technology, literature, philosophy, mathematics, and art, among other fields. Germany was fertile ground for intellectuals, artists, and innovators. What this should tell the world is if such a well-educated population can be so thoroughly brainwashed, then virtually everyone is vulnerable to being brainwashed.

The Third Reich demonstrated how a well-developed propaganda campaign can be more effective than any weapon in the subjugation of an entire population. Hitler had the entire population mesmerized and hanging on his every word. There isn't a government or military in the world that wouldn't want this kind of power and control. The power of propaganda, the power of persuasion, is more effective than the barrel of a gun. Complete conformity of the population is the goal, and when this is achieved, there will be no more resistance.

It turns out President Truman's concerns about the CIA were well founded. By the 1950s the agency launched a top-secret program called Operation Mockingbird, which actively sought to influence and manipulate the mainstream media. The agency placed assets in domestic and international news organizations to plant CIA-written propaganda stories in the newspapers and wire services read by the public at home and abroad. In other cases, the agency outright bribed journalists and publishers. Some of the nation's most respected newspapers and publications either knowingly or unknowingly participated: *New York Times*, *The Washington Post*, *Newsweek*, *Time Magazine*, CBS, ABC, the Associated Press, United Press International, Reuters, Hearst Newspapers, *Miami Herald*, and *New York Herald-Tribune*, among nearly forty others. Operation Mockingbird was eventually discovered by the press and was disbanded, but it is suspected, like all secret programs that get revealed, that they eventually get relaunched under a different name at a later date.

It shouldn't be a surprise at how easy it was to compromise the journalistic integrity and impartiality of the corporate-owned news media. After all, these corporations stood to reap massive profits from the escalation of the Cold War, so they didn't hesitate to report whatever the CIA and military told them to report. This is why the public is so misinformed about the current state of affairs, because the lackey news media is subservient to the interests of corporations.

These agency propaganda specialists push their agenda at every turn, without the media even realizing that they're being manipulated. They meet regularly with Hollywood and network executives to pitch certain ideas or plots for television shows and movies. The CIA and military have briefings with the press in order to put out the stories they want reported. This manipulation is so subtle that it's difficult to detect; yet on a subliminal or subconscious level, it's shaping people's behavior and beliefs. These invisible influences are everywhere.

In addition to the propaganda efforts of the CIA, the agency also soon exploited a loophole in its charter that allowed it to launch in 1959 its first domestic operation in response to the agency's need to identify and recruit anti-Castro Cuban exiles who resided in the United States and who could assist the agency in their efforts against Fidel Castro. A few years later, in 1964, President Lyndon Johnson formally established the Domestic Operations Division. This laid the groundwork for the CIA to launch its first domestic "espionage" operation with the aim of infiltrating college campuses across America in order to learn whether foreign influences were behind the student antiwar movement that opposed the Vietnam War. With a foothold in domestic operations, the CIA never looked back.

Since being founded back in 1947, the CIA has metastasized throughout government at all levels. It has set up interagency exchange programs in which it loans agency employees to other government and law enforcement agencies at the federal, state, and even local levels. In other cases it simply recruits personnel from these various organizations to assist with the CIA's domestic policing and surveillance programs. Bottom line, the CIA is everywhere.

20

DICK WORTHINGTON, WHOSE father had been one of the OSS's first recruits, was recruited by the CIA while attending Yale Law School. Upon graduation in 1963, Dick joined the agency's Clandestine Services and had been with the agency ever since.

At the time Dick joined the agency, there was intense pressure from the CIA and military for an increase in US involvement in Vietnam. Vietnam had been a colonial possession of France for nearly the past hundred years, but after their crushing defeat at Dien Bien Phu in 1954, the French hastily withdrew from Vietnam in order to focus on the growing insurgency closer to home in another of their colonial possessions, Algeria. The CIA and US military were determined to fill the void left by France in Vietnam. Their argument was if America didn't fill the political and military vacuum in Vietnam, the Soviets would take advantage of the situation and use it as an opportunity to expand throughout Southeast Asia—the domino theory, as it was known.

When President Kennedy took office in January 1961, the outgoing President Eisenhower (retired five-star World War II general who served as the supreme commander of the Allied forces in Europe) had cautioned President Kennedy about the unbridled power and influence of the CIA and military. President Kennedy would learn firsthand about the CIA when it launched the bungled Bay of Pigs in April 1961 to invade the island nation of Cuba to overthrow Fidel Castro. President Kennedy knew that he was being manipulated by the CIA and military. At one point President Kennedy even threatened to "splinter the CIA into a thousand pieces."

President Kennedy heeded the advice of former President Eisenhower and did not, despite the unrelenting pressure by the CIA and military, send troops to Vietnam. However, in an effort to placate the war mongers, President Kennedy did send a handful of special advisers to the country in 1963. This wasn't good enough, as the CIA and military wanted all-out war in this far-away, unheard-of country in Southeast Asia. On November 22, 1963, the nation's first Catholic President was assassinated. Vice President Johnson was then sworn in as president, and he gave the green light for an escalation of what was then the conflict in Vietnam, which turned out to be one of America's greatest foreign-policy debacles.

Dick Worthington was one of the special advisers who was sent to Vietnam in 1963. In his first assignment at the agency, Dick's role was to help set up the agency's Phoenix Program, which was a torture and assassination program that targeted the opposition Viet Cong guerrillas in the south and the Ho Chi Minh Communists in the north. The program was operational from 1965 to 1972 and killed an estimated thirty-five thousand enemy Vietnamese. Enemy body counts were the flawed method of determining the success of operations in Vietnam. During the course of the war, over one million enemy Vietnamese were killed compared to fifty-eight thousand American soldiers, yet few would say the war was a US victory.

Some years later, with several assignments in between, Dick would achieve legendary status within the agency for his work in Afghanistan. Dick worked with the mujahideen fighters in their war against the Soviet invaders. The CIA's involvement in Afghanistan was payback to the Soviets for their role in arming America's enemies in both the Korean and Vietnam wars. Dick arrived in Afghanistan at the height of the war in the mid-1980s. At that time, the armored Soviet Hind attack helicopters, which were impervious to small-arms fire, maintained absolute control of the skies, which allowed them to wreak havoc on the mujahideen fighters and civilians on the ground with impunity.

That all changed in October 1986, when Dick was able to deliver the first of hundreds of Stinger missiles to the mujahideen. The Stingers were shoulder-fired surface-to-air missiles with an infrared homing system that had a range of up to five miles. These missiles were capable of shooting down Soviet aircraft, most important of which was the much-feared Hind armored attack gunship, whose official name was Mi-24, dubbed "Satan's Chariot." The arrival of the Stinger missiles sent shock waves throughout the Soviet military and marked the beginning of the end of the Soviet Union's war in Afghanistan. Without Soviet air power in the skies, supply convoys couldn't be protected, which also meant that ground troops were also left helpless when ambushed. Needless to say that Soviet casualties quickly escalated from this point forward and culminated with the Soviet's withdrawal in defeat in 1989.

Dick had earned the respect and trust of his agency colleagues because of his vast field experience. The field person knows all too well how the best-planned operation can still fall apart in a myriad of unforeseen ways. Nothing is black and white; everything is gray.

The field person's axiom says that with field experience comes fail-ure, with failure comes humility, with humility comes wisdom. That axiom also applies to countries. People who are successful know full well not to underestimate the value of failure. The people who are dreaded the most are the ones who have never taken up a chal-lenge outside of their comfort zone at headquarters. Yet ironically it's these people with the least amount of experience who are the ones that think they have all the answers.

After all the years in the field, Dick wanted to finish out his career with the agency on home soil, and when offered the position of Deputy Director of the Northeast Regional Domestic Operations Division, he jumped at the opportunity. He was considered a good choice by agency insiders because of his sound judgment and the ability to get the job done, which was exactly what was needed to coordinate activities on US soil.

The CIA's Northeast Regional Offices were located in Lower Manhattan on the twenty-fifth floor of 7 World Trade Center. The CIA shared the twenty-fifth floor with the Department of Defense and the IRS. The World Trade Center, with its stumpy forty-seven floors, often went unnoticed in the shadow of the Twin Towers, which reached upward of 110 floors.

The CIA offices were ideal for debriefing American executives returning from overseas business trips who were willing to provide details of their business activities, and in return the CIA would pro-vide them with intelligence on their foreign corporate competitors. It was a mutually beneficial relationship. The offices were also well situated for spying on and recruiting foreign diplomats assigned to the United Nations and the hundreds of foreign diplomatic missions located throughout New York City.

This day was going to be different for Dick. Two days earlier he had been contacted by someone he knew was associated with the more shadowy side of the agency. Dick was informed about an SVR operation involving a Russian traitor and an American woman by the name of Nathalie Rosenfeld. Dick had no direct role in the operation, but was aware just in case support of any kind was needed. The Russians were professionals, so it wasn't likely there would be any problems, but Dick would be there to coordinate whatever support necessary.

Dick was expecting a telephone call from the SVR team leader, Victor Yurchenko, when the operation was over and the team had safely returned to their warehouse in Brighton Beach.

The secure telephone on Dick's desk rang.

"Hello, Mr. CIA." Just ten years after the Soviets withdrew from Afghanistan in defeat, Victor found himself cooperating with his agency's nemesis, the CIA. What Victor didn't share was that he knew it was Dick who delivered the Afghans with the Stinger missiles that killed his countrymen. *The world of intelligence makes for strange bedfellows*, thought Victor.

"Hello, Victor," replied Dick, "how did everything go?"

"As you Americans say, it went like clockwork," said Victor. "We have our much-surprised Russian traitor in custody. His name is Vasili Borisovich; he works at the Kremlin Archives."

Dick already knew that but didn't betray his foreknowledge.

"We have his hotel-room key from the Marriott Hotel in Times Square. Two of our team are on their way there now to clear out his belongings. I'll be interrogating him shortly to learn the rest. As for the Rosenfeld woman, you'll never have to worry about her again. We were also able to recover the photographs," said Victor.

"I guess you don't even need my help," said Dick.

"Well, Dick, everything went well, but there was just one thing."

"What is it?" asked Dick.

"There was a witness. He saw everything."

"I'm listening," said Dick.

Victor went on to describe the events that took place inside the restaurant and sidewalk afterward.

"Describe what he looked like," Dick said, as he leaned back in his chair to listen with his undivided attention.

Victor described the witness. "He was in his late twenties and wore a dark-blue suit and overcoat. When I first saw him, I thought he looked like one of your FBI guys. Clearly he wasn't though, given how he reacted to the woman's death. When he knelt beside her, he seemed deeply saddened, as if he knew the woman. He didn't try to pursue our guy; he was only interested in the woman. Two of my team followed him when he left the scene, but they lost sight of him in the holiday crowd at Rockefeller Center.

"My team is absolutely convinced that this witness didn't know her and was in the restaurant merely by coincidence. His decision to follow seemed spur-of-the-moment," said Victor, trying to sound confident in his words. "He seemed unsure about whether or not to follow."

After a few moments of silence, Dick spoke. "We don't need to worry. Worst-case scenario, if this witness comes forward, I'll just have to get our FBI person involved, as was the contingency anyhow. The FBI can then take over jurisdiction of the case from NYPD on national security grounds. They'll then make sure the investigation goes nowhere. It's that simple."

"Okay, that sounds good. I have pictures of the witness that I can e-mail to you. I snapped a few when he was approaching the restaurant and also when he left following the woman."

"Why did you take a picture of him entering the restaurant when at that point you didn't even know he was involved?" asked Dick.

"I don't know. There was something about him that caught my attention. Like I said, he looked like an FBI guy; that must have been what caught my attention," explained Victor.

The fact that Victor had taken a picture of the witness before the witness even became a witness triggered an alarm for Dick. As a field guy, Dick had learned to always trust his intuition. Something wasn't right. Dick knew this detail changed everything. The first thing he needed to do was put a name to the face. Only then could he rule out the witness's involvement as coincidence.

"Victor, send the pictures to my e-mail address. I'm going to run them against the agency database just to be thorough, and I suggest you do the same on your side," stated Dick.

"Okay. I'll do the same," said Victor.

"Call again as soon as you learn anything, and I'll do the same," said Dick. Then without a good-bye, but with contemplation, he slowly lowered the telephone receiver to the cradle.

21

EVEN IF THE precinct building hadn't been surrounded by police cars, it still would have been easy to spot. The building was little more than heap of raw concrete. The precinct had such a cold and unwelcoming feeling to it. During the 1950s and 1960s, many government buildings around the United States and Europe were designed in this brutalist architectural style. There was nothing esthetically redeeming about the building, but it was functional and thus served its purpose.

I arrived at the precinct shortly after two o'clock and introduced myself to the desk sergeant, who then directed me to the waiting area and told me that a detective would be with me shortly. There were about ten other people seated in the waiting area. *What brought these other people to the Eighteenth Precinct on this snowy December day?* I wondered. One of them was an African-American woman. She must have been someone's mother or grandmother. I would guess she was there not for something she had done but for someone else. She looked down at her lap the entire time, not looking up even once. Her faced seemed drained of emotion, more than just being sad. As hard as life can be, it can be infinitely harder for others.

That thought made me reflective, and my attention returned to the mystery woman. I still couldn't grasp the reality that one minute she was so alive and filled with purpose, and then minutes later she was killed right before my eyes. That strange feeling of being pulled to follow her—maybe I was supposed to bear witness to her death. It made no sense, but that was exactly how it felt.

"David Walker?" asked someone wearing a sport coat, with a badge and holster attached to his belt.

I instinctively raised my hand but then quickly withdrew it, but not before the detective noticed. "Yes, I'm David."

"I'm Detective Lorenzo; come with me." There was no handshake.

Detective Anthony Lorenzo was a third-generation civil servant in New York City. His father and grandfather had worked at the Department of Sanitation, but Anthony wanted to be a policeman. After receiving his college degree in criminal justice, he joined the NYPD at the age of twenty-five. Anthony had been with the force for the past sixteen years and received his long-sought-after promotion to detective four years ago. He was a second-generation Long Islander, married to his high-school sweetheart. They had two boys, ages nine and eleven. He was raising his family in the same town in which he grew up.

I followed the detective into a small interview room. Well, for me it was an interview room, but I guess if I was on the other side of the law, it would be an interrogation room. Anyhow, in the room there was a wooden table and two chairs, and on the wall there was a telephone that looked like it had been there ever since the concrete was poured. The room was typical of something that would have been depicted on the older television police dramas such as *Hill Street Blues* or even earlier on *Barney Miller.*

The detective walked to the far side of the table to sit in the chair facing the door and gestured with his hand for me to sit in the chair on the opposite side.

"Thank you for coming in, Mr. Walker. The desk sergeant said you wanted to speak to someone about the woman who died on Forty-Eighth Street."

"Yes, that is right, Detective."

"Before we get started, let me take down your personal information," said the detective as he reached for his notebook.

"Detective, if you don't mind, could you tell me the name of the woman?"

He looked me in the eyes long and hard before he answered. "Her name was Nathalie Rosenfeld. She was twenty-nine years old."

She was only two years younger than me. Her name confirmed why she was wearing a Jewish star pendant, not that it meant anything; it was merely an observation.

After a slight pause, he opened his notebook and said my name aloud, "David Walker," as he wrote it on a blank page. "Do you have identification with you?"

"Yes, here is my driver's license."

"You're from Rhode Island?"

"Yes, I moved to Manhattan almost two years ago."

"You're required to have a New York driver's license if you live here," stated the detective.

"I didn't know that. I'll be sure to get one now that I know," I responded.

The detective gave me a look before copying down the information on my license. He then proceeded to ask my current employer and address, apartment address, and my cell phone number.

"The desk sergeant told me that you saw something suspicious before Ms. Rosenfeld collapsed."

"Yes, I did."

"Tell me what it is you think you may have seen." The detective seemed like a cynic, but I imagine he hears lots of things, so he needs to be circumspect with witness statements and be careful not to allow himself to be taken on some wild goose chase that leads nowhere.

I recounted the events from the moment I entered Au Bon Pain up until returning to my office, the detective's face betraying no emotion. Occasionally he jotted something down in his notebook, but otherwise he maintained eye contact with me the entire time. When I was finished sharing what I had witnessed, he followed up with a few questions.

"Why were you watching Ms. Rosenfeld in the first place?"

"Like I said, Detective, she just stood out from everyone," I replied. "She didn't blend with the crowd. There was an aura about her. Plus, she was stunningly beautiful, not supermodel beautiful but deeper."

"Forgive me for practicing what little French I learned in high school, but do you mean something like a *je ne sais quoi*? This is what the French refer to as the intangible of having that something special about someone that sets that person apart from the rest."

"Not exactly, unless the 'something special' is multiplied by ten and added to it was a sense of purpose."

The detective's brow furrowed, conveying that he understood precisely the image I was trying to convey.

"Tell me, David, how is it that someone who sells voice mail knows so much about women's fashion?"

"I didn't know this much about women's fashion until I moved to Manhattan. Now, every day on my walk to work, from the Upper East Side to my office on Fifth Avenue in Midtown, I pass some of the most exclusive clothing and jewelry stores in the world. Bergdorf Goodman, Saks Fifth Avenue, Henri Bendel, Barneys of New York, Bloomingdales, Macy's, high-end European clothing boutiques, Cartier, Tiffany, Harry Winston, DeBeers, and countless others. As just an ordinary passerby, I can't help but notice the storefront displays, and that's why I'm so informed of women's fashion and style." I knew my overly thorough answer entirely answered the detective's question.

It seemed like the detective was trying to gauge my credibility. He trusted what I was saying, but he was just being cautious, as detectives are.

"Why did you decide to follow her?" asked the detective.

"My curiosity just got the better of me, I suppose. I was intrigued by her presence in the first place. Then I saw her and the Russian exchange the subtle nods before he approached and passed her the envelope. The whole encounter between the two of them was just too intriguing for me not to have followed."

"Tell me more about the man who you think killed Nathalie."

"There's not much more to say. His entire outfit was a dark monotone, and he was wearing a fedora that covered his eyes as he approached. I think his outfit was black, but sometimes I get black and dark blue confused, depending on the lighting. When he stepped into her path, his left hand was already raised and angled to her face. He stepped close to her chest and whispered something to her. She took one, maybe two, steps forward, then collapsed like a ballerina. It was after he removed the envelope from her handbag and stood that he made eye contact with me. I'll never forget his ice-cold blue eyes. I guarantee that was not the first time he killed. I'm certain of it."

"Did this man also look Russian?" asked the detective.

"I'm fairly certain the guy from inside the restaurant was Russian, but I'm not sure about the killer," I said. "But he definitely looked foreign."

"Detective, can I hazard a guess as to how she was killed?"

The detective gave me an incredulous look, dropped his pen on his notebook, and leaned back in his chair as if waiting to be entertained. "Go right ahead."

"Detective, admittedly, I read many spy novels. Perhaps too many for my own good, but that's what I enjoy reading. Some of these novels are written very true to life. In the books, when the Russians want to kill someone discreetly to make it look as though the person died of natural causes, they use some type of cyanide aerosol spray. When sprayed into the person's face, the cyanide is inhaled and immediately enters the bloodstream and goes to the heart and causes the person to go into instant cardiac arrest. The cyanide dissipates quickly in the bloodstream, leaving no trace, which makes it impossible to test for afterward through toxicology tests, which normally don't even test for cyanide anyway. This is what the Russians do. For the record, the CIA has its own heart-attack gun that shoots a tiny poisonous dart into a person, which also causes a heart attack. The point is, these agencies have ways to kill people and make it look like the person died of natural causes."

"You know all that from reading novels?" asked the detective, with the most disbelieving look on his face.

"Yes, that is correct. When I knelt beside her, there were no signs whatsoever that she was killed. But I'm certain the killer's left hand was raised toward her face. He could have easily had something concealed under the sleeve of his coat."

It was hard for the detective to accept my theory, but I could see that he was trying to connect the dots.

"David, let's not get ahead of ourselves," said the detective. "If you don't mind, I'd like to have you sit down with our artist to draw up a composite sketch of the man who bumped into Ms. Rosenfeld."

"Okay."

He stood and walked over the telephone on the wall—for internal calls only—and keyed in a four-digit extension. "Diane, are you free? I have a witness here, and we need to prepare a likeness." Pause. "Terrific; I'll walk him up."

After he hung up the telephone but before he could say anything, there was a quick knock on the door. Then the door opened, and the desk sergeant's head peered inside.

"Detective, can I have a word with you?"

I couldn't hear what they were saying, but after a few seconds, the detective came back in and said that he needed to make a telephone call and that the sergeant would escort me to the sketch artist. "When you're done, she'll bring you back to me, and we'll finish up," said the detective.

22

DETECTIVE LORENZO RETURNED to his desk and dialed the telephone number that was given to him by the desk sergeant for the emergency room at Mount Sinai Hospital. "Hello, can I speak with Dr. Leventhal? I'm returning his call."

"Hello, Doctor, I'm Detective Lorenzo from the Eighteenth Precinct in Midtown. You called a few minutes ago?"

"Yes, I did. I called about the twenty-nine-year-old woman named Nathalie Rosenfeld. She arrived DOA at the emergency room a short while ago. I was the doctor who attended to her. It appeared that Ms. Rosenfeld died of a massive cardiac arrest. There's nothing to indicate any sign of foul play. The reason I called you, however, is because her father is here at the hospital. He's convinced that she was killed. He said that his daughter had a meeting with a Russian man today and is convinced that she was killed."

The fact that she had a meeting with a Russian captured the detective's attention, knowing that the witness had described the man from inside the restaurant as Russian.

"Doctor, is the woman's father still there?"

"Yes, he's in the other room."

"Would you be able to put him on the telephone for a moment? I need to speak to him."

"Sure, Detective, wait one moment and I'll get him for you."

There were about ten seconds of silence, then a voice said, "Hello, this is Claude Rosenfeld speaking."

"Hello, Mr. Rosenfeld, I'm Detective Anthony Lorenzo. I'm very sorry about the death of your daughter."

"Thank you, Detective."

"The doctor mentioned that you believe your daughter might have been killed."

"Yes, I'm certain of it. She was supposed to meet with a Russian today; it must have been him."

"There's a witness at the precinct now. He already gave a statement. Could we meet for a few minutes?"

"That isn't a problem. I'm leaving the hospital shortly and heading to my art and antique gallery where some friends and family will be gathering. I have an office there where we can talk."

After giving the address to the detective, Claude put the doctor back on the telephone.

"Doctor, when will the autopsy be conducted?" asked the detective.

"We already called the medical examiner (ME) to pick up the body. They should be on their way as we speak. They are the ones who will perform the autopsy, and they'll conduct toxicology testing."

"Thanks for your time, Doctor. I'll give the ME a call. Thanks for the call, Dr. Leventhal."

After the detective ended the call, he dialed the ME's office.

"Hello, this is Detective Lorenzo from the Eighteenth Precinct. Can I speak to Dr. Carlisle?"

"Yes, Detective, please hold a moment."

"Hello, Detective Lorenzo. It's been quite some time since the last time we spoke. How can I help you?"

"I'm calling about a twenty-nine-year-old woman who went into cardiac arrest today and died. She's at Mount Sinai Hospital's emergency room now, and I believe your office has already sent a vehicle to pick up her body. Her name is Nathalie Rosenfeld."

"Hang on; let me check the computer. Yes, she's in our system. A vehicle is on the way to the hospital now," replied Dr. Carlisle.

"Okay. I'm calling because she may have been killed in a way that is not easily detectable. The police at the scene didn't notice any signs of foul play and neither did the doctor from the Mount Sinai emergency room. But I have a witness who claims to have seen a man bump into the woman, and he thinks the man may have sprayed something into her face seconds before she collapsed. Her father is at the emergency room, and he is also convinced that she was killed."

"What is it you want from me, Detective?"

"Doctor, I need you to perform a thorough battery of toxicology tests on the Rosenfeld woman, beyond the normal scope of testing. If she was killed, it is possible whatever was used will be difficult to detect." The detective was reluctant to even ask, but he forced out the question. "Doctor, would it be possible for you to test for cyanide poisoning?"

"I can. We usually don't test for that, but I can order a separate test if you want," replied the doctor.

"Yes, Doctor, please do. There may be Russian involvement on this case, and I recall reading before that Russians sometimes use a cyanide spray to kill their dissidents living abroad."

"I'll be sure to order that test for you, Detective. But it is difficult to test for, as it denatures quickly once it enters the body, thus leaving no trace."

"So I've heard. How soon before you're able to perform the autopsy and toxicology testing?"

"We can complete the autopsy tonight and have preliminary results available within the next few days, but the toxicology results will not be available for a month at the earliest. Until we have those toxicology results, an official cause of death cannot be determined. I'll call you as soon as I learn anything," said the doctor.

"Thank you, Dr. Carlisle. I'll be in touch as well."

The detective considered his next move. He then reached for the telephone receiver and dialed the extension for the desk sergeant.

"Sarge, can you send someone to Au Bon Pain on Forty-Eighth Street near Rockefeller Plaza?"

"Sure, what do you need?"

"I need copies of the security tapes from ten a.m. to two p.m. today. I also need footage from any cameras outside on Forty-Eighth Street between Fifth Avenue and Times Square."

"I'll send someone out immediately," replied the sergeant.

"Thanks."

23

I FINISHED WITH the police sketch artist at three thirty, and then she walked me to the detective's desk.

"Here's your man," said Diane as she handed the composite sketch to the detective.

"Thanks, Diane. You're the best," said the detective, with a slight smile.

While walking away, she casually looked back over her should and playfully said, "Yeah, yeah. You're welcome."

"This is the guy you think killed her?" asked the detective.

"That's him," I said.

The detective then fed the sketch into a scanner on the filing cabinet next to his desk.

"What are you doing?" I asked.

"I'm scanning the likeness into the database so I can attach it to Ms. Rosenfeld's file."

The detective then sat down at his desk and opened his notebook and began entering information from one of the pages into the system as well. I peered at the open page and noticed it was my name and biographical information that he was entering into the system.

"Detective, you're adding my name to Nathalie's file? Are you sure that's okay?"

"What do you mean? Of course it's okay. I'm just adding you as a witness."

I knew this wasn't a good idea. "Detective, when I was in the restaurant, I had a feeling that maybe everything was under surveillance. It was just a feeling, but what if the handoff was under surveillance? What if this is bigger than we realize?"

"David, the information is secure in our systems. You're being paranoid. Nobody is going to learn your identity, so you have nothing to worry about."

"Detective, I'm just trying to be careful."

There was no dissuading him from entering the information. All I could do was sit in silence while he finished updating Nathalie's file.

When he was finished, he leaned back in his chair and told me that I was free to leave the precinct. If anything came up, he would give me a call.

"Now that my name is out there, what if the killer somehow learns my identity? The killer was serious when he made eye contact before leaving the scene. What if he's trying to find me?"

"David, you're making more out of this than is warranted. You'll be safe. Just go home and get a good night's sleep. It's been a long day for you," said the detective, in a slightly patronizing tone.

"What are you doing after I leave?"

"While you were upstairs with Diane, I briefly spoke to Nathalie's father on the telephone. I'm going to talk to him at the family's art gallery. By the way, it looks like you were right. Her father confirmed that his daughter was meeting with a Russian today at Au Bon Pain."

"I knew he was a Russian, but thanks for confirming. If you could, Detective, mention to Nathalie's father that if possible, I'd like to meet him at some point. As the last person to see her alive, I think maybe he'd also appreciate speaking to me."

"I'll mention it. In the meantime, here's my card. I wrote my cell phone number on the back. If anything comes up, just call me."

"Detective, if anything comes up, it's going to be too late to call you."

"David, everything's going to be okay. I'll call you tomorrow. Try not to think about it tonight."

"Okay, we'll talk tomorrow," I replied, but I was convinced the detective was entirely underestimating the situation.

24

THE NYPD'S DATABASE, like the databases from all local, state, and federal law enforcement agencies across the country, feeds into the FBI's National Crime Information Center (NCIC) database, which is the central repository for all criminal records in the United States. When Detective Lorenzo updated Nathalie Rosenfeld's file, that information was immediately updated in the NCIC database. Because Nathalie Rosenfeld was on the CIA's watch list, the CIA was immediately alerted to the update.

Dick Worthington was reviewing the pictures of the witness that he received from Victor when his computer pinged to alert him that the Rosenfeld file had been updated. When he clicked on Nathalie's file, the first thing he saw was the sketch of the SVR's assassin. All Dick could do was to shake his head. The reason for using the cyanide spray to kill her in the first place was so that she could be killed in a way to make it look like she died of natural causes. Nobody was supposed to know that a crime had even been committed. Now suddenly the NYPD had a sketch of the assassin.

Dick continued to read the file and noted that the name David Walker had been added to the file as a witness. Dick double clicked on the witness's name, and the picture from his Rhode Island driver's license popped up on the screen along with his biographical information. Dick immediately recognized that the picture staring at him on his computer screen was the same person in the pictures he received from Victor. There was no longer a need to run the picture of the witness through the agency's facial recognition system for identification.

The good news was that the witness had been identified. The bad news was that the witness's statement to the police meant that the NYPD would now have to investigate. As inconvenient as it was to have this witness to the murder, Dick felt the situation was still under control. Worst-case scenario they have to bring the FBI into the loop; then they could take jurisdiction of the Rosenfeld case on national-security grounds. This was the most effective way to shut down the NYPD case.

Dick thought that the witness going to the police was actually a good sign. If Walker had been involved in the operation in any way whatsoever, he wouldn't have gone to the police. Dick still thought it prudent to run Walker's name against the CIA's database, just in case.

Dick couldn't believe his eyes when the database came back with a match. Not only was this David Walker in the system, but just like Nathalie, he was also on the agency's watch list. All Dick could manage to do was lower his face into his hands and under his breath murmur to himself, "What the fuck is going on?"

25

AS FAR BACK as David Walker could remember, there was something about his elderly German neighbors that put him on edge. That wasn't entirely surprising, given that the neighbors were often yelling at David and his brother, Todd, and sisters, along with all the neighborhood children, for doing nothing more than just being kids. But that wasn't what unnerved David about his neighbors. There was something else.

Whenever David was in their presence, he sensed an eerie coldness about them that made the hair on the back of his neck stand on edge. The feeling was palpable. He mentioned this unease about his neighbors to his parents, but they merely dismissed his concerns without a second thought.

It was when David reached high school and learned about US history, in particular about World War II, that the mystery of his neighbors began to reveal itself. Simple math allowed David to estimate that the husband would have been in his mid- to late twenties at the start of World War II in September of 1939, which meant it was very likely he served in the Third Reich in some capacity. David was convinced that the unsettling vibe that surrounded his neighbors had everything to do with what the husband had done during the war.

The narrative that the couple had circulated was that they were in Germany during the war and then emigrated to the United States in the early 1950s with their two children. They always made a point of making it clear that the husband had not been in the military but worked as a jet propulsion engineer for a German company. This made sense given the fact that the husband was working in Rhode Island for the subsidiary of the German Hoechst Corporation, which was a military defense contractor. The story seemed plausible, but David suspected it wasn't the truth.

What David could never reconcile was that despite the horrendous atrocities committed by Germany during the war, the couple seemed very proud of their German heritage. There were no signs of remorse. Even if they had no direct role in the war, how could they not bear some of the shame for the Holocaust and the death and destruction inflicted across Europe by their country? In fact, when David would observe the German couple walking around the neighborhood, he always thought and even used to tell his parents his neighbors "carried themselves as if the Nazis had won the war, not lost it."

As an avid reader of the *New York Times*, a habit he picked up as a newspaper delivery boy at the age of twelve, David came across a newspaper article in 1985 when he was seventeen years old about the work of the Simon Wiesenthal Center (SWC) in Los Angeles. The center's namesake was himself a Holocaust survivor from the Mauthausen concentration camp in Austria. After the war, he committed his life to avenging the deaths of the six million Jews who perished in the Nazi death camps. It became his life's mission to help track down and bring to justice the Nazi war criminals who escaped

Germany at the end of the war and were now living freely in the United States and around the globe. The SWC has been responsible for bringing to justice over a thousand Nazi war criminals.

The most notorious of them was Adolf Eichmann, who was a lieutenant colonel in the SS under Heinrich Himmler. Eichmann was the person in charge of the deportations of the Jewish population to the Nazi death camps. Simon Wiesenthal had learned that Adolf Eichmann was living freely in Argentina. He then shared the information with the Israeli Mossad. The Mossad, without informing the Argentine government, carried out a daring operation in 1960 in which Adolf Eichmann was kidnapped and flown to Israel, where he stood trial for crimes against humanity and crimes against the Jewish people. Eichmann was convicted and hanged in 1962.

Convinced that his German neighbor was one of these Nazi war criminals living in plain sight, David decided to call the Nazi hunters at the SWC. As far as David was concerned, regardless of the fact that forty years had passed since the end of World War II, if his neighbor was responsible for any of the atrocities committed during the war, then he should have to answer for those crimes. *It was a matter of principle*, he thought.

When David called the SWC, he spoke to an investigator who referred to himself as a researcher. The researcher was fairly matter of fact, taking down the name of the neighbor, estimated age, and the home address. David also shared the family's narrative. The researcher told David that he would look into the matter and give him a call back in a few weeks to share whatever was learned about the neighbor.

After several months without a return phone call, David called the researcher back and asked for an update. This time the investigator wasn't polite, but was curt to the point of being rude. The man told David that his neighbor was clean and that there was no basis for his suspicions and insinuated that he shouldn't have called the center with such a frivolous call. The conversation lasted less than thirty seconds. David was caught off guard by the researcher's behavior. But more significantly, he had been so convinced of his neighbor's guilt, but yet he was told that his neighbor was clean. David had no idea how he got it so wrong. Every bone in his body had told him his neighbor was guilty of something, but he knew he had to defer to the SWC investigator.

What David had no way of knowing was that the SWC had a secret agreement with the US Justice Department that prohibited the center from confirming his suspicions about his neighbor. This agreement strictly prohibited the center from pursuing or releasing any information on any German who had been brought to the United States as part of a US-government-sanctioned operation. David's neighbor and his family were covered under this agreement, as they had been resettled in America after the war under the OSS/CIA Operation Paperclip. To ensure that the SWC honored its agreement, the NSA monitored all telephone calls, electronic communications, and mail to and from the center. The SWC had to honor this agreement, as it was the cost of being able to operate on US soil. But the center did share everything with the Israeli government.

The SWC was well aware of the identity of David's neighbor. In fact, the center was deliberately rude to David in order to deter him from following up on his neighbor any further. It was done for his own safety. What the center knew but didn't share about David's neighbor was that he was a notorious Nazi war criminal who served in the SS and reported directly to Heinrich Himmler, the man considered the architect of the Holocaust. Despite being one of the most wanted, he and his family were resettled in the United States after the war.

David's telephone call to the SWC had been intercepted by the NSA. The NSA then sent a report that included the transcript of the conversation to the CIA, where it was directed to an office at the agency that dealt with matters concerning Nazis. It turns out David's neighbor was no ordinary SS officer. He was part of an underground cell of SS officers dispatched to the United States after the war as one of the conspirators in Hitler's secret plot against America. That was how at the age of seventeen years old, David Walker became one of the youngest people ever to earn a place on the CIA's watch list forever.

Part 2

26

IT WAS WITH incredulous disbelief that Dick Worthington read David Walker's file. Nobody could have ever imagined that the operation could have gotten any more complicated than it had just become. Not only was David Walker on the agency's watch list, but the reason he was on the list in the first place was because of a telephone call he made back in 1985 to the Nazi hunters at the SWC to report his suspicions that his German neighbor was a Nazi war criminal.

In an impossible-to-dismiss coincidence, Walker's neighbor was one of the account holders on a secret list of accounts that got Nathalie killed. Intelligence officers don't believe in coincidences, which meant Dick no longer had the luxury of dismissing Walker as a curious bystander. He now had to accept the very real likelihood that David and Nathalie had been working together.

David's neighbor was also in the database, but when Dick double-clicked on the file, he was denied access. This wasn't unusual given how the CIA, like all intelligence agencies, compartmentalized its intelligence to ensure that no one person can glean too much about the agency's activities. It's also an effective way to hide the agency's agenda.

The next surprise came as Dick scanned the names of Walker's family, friends, and associates. One name in particular jumped out. "I don't believe this. What a small world," Dick said, in a soft mumble. For the second time in two minutes, Dick found himself shaking his head in disbelief. The name that caught Dick's attention was that of a man his father had introduced him to at an agency reception nearly three decades earlier, in the early 1970s. Dick remembered the man, not because decades later he would be elected governor of Rhode Island but because of how highly his father had spoken of him. The future governor had been a B-17 bomber pilot during World War II. On his return from a bombing mission over Germany, the Luftwaffe shot down his plane over Nazi-occupied Belgium. Several of the crew were killed when the B-17 was strafed by the German fighters, and the remaining crew parachuted safely but were quickly captured by German soldiers and spent the rest of the war in a POW camp. The future governor was the only one who was able to evade capture. He made his way to France, where he established contact with the French Resistance and eventually made his way to neutral Switzerland. Once in Switzerland, he was recruited by the OSS and then returned to occupied France, where once again he joined up with the French Resistance and wreaked havoc behind enemy lines for the remainder of the war. "A true war hero," Dick recalled his father saying of the man.

It turned out that David Walker, in his first job out of college, had been a staffer for the governor. The file showed that the two remained in contact after the governor left office and for the past two years had been in a relationship with the governor's daughter. This development changed absolutely everything.

As Dick continued reading through Walker's file, it turned out that David had met with an agency recruiter a few years earlier. At the time the agency wasn't hiring because of severe budget cuts under the Clinton administration, but when Walker reached out to the agency, they thought it would be the perfect opportunity to meet the person who had unknowingly stumbled upon the agency's darkest secret.

The interview went very well, and as a result Walker was invited to complete an application for employment with the agency. He applied for the overseas Clandestine Services but lacked any relevant experience to be considered for a covert-operative position. However, having demonstrated a solid understanding of world events and history, the agency was interested in him for an analyst position. In applying to the CIA, Walker had to sign a waiver that allowed the agency to conduct a thorough and in-depth background check on the candidate. Agency investigators spoke to references and neighbors. Between the interview and the background check, the agency was able to confirm that he matched his NSA profile. Nothing of significance turned up, but it gave the CIA another layer to his file. He was basically a history buff and someone who's curious and asks lots of questions.

The CIA planned on hiring Walker once funding was restored. Unbeknown to Walker, after completion of the background check, the agency had issued him provisional security clearance so that when funding was restored he could be hired immediately. However, funding wouldn't be restored until President George W. Bush took office in 2001. As a result, not being able to wait forever, David withdrew his application and went into the financial-services sector.

When Dick Worthington was contacted by the shadow group at the agency about the Rosenfeld Operation, he was entrusted to handle matters on his own. The killing of an American on US soil is about as sensitive as it gets. It knew Dick had the judgment to handle the matter on his own without its interference. The group also wanted to limit its exposure. The key to plausible deniability is that there is a complete lack of evidence to make it easy for someone to deny knowledge of the actions committed by another person, usually a subordinate. The group didn't want to hear back from Dick until all matters were resolved.

In the criminal-justice system, there is a presumption of innocence of the accused, but in the field of intelligence, coincidences are tantamount to a presumption of guilt, unless proven otherwise. However, in this situation, Dick was prepared to go against his better judgment and give Walker the benefit of the doubt. He did this not for David per se but out of respect to the man his father had introduced him to at that agency reception some thirty years earlier. If however, indisputable evidence surfaced, proving that the Rosenfeld woman and Walker had in fact been working together, then there would be nothing more he could do for the not-so-coincidental witness. And that was how, in a bizarre twist of circumstances, Dick Worthington would become David Walker's self-appointed protector.

27

BY THE TIME I left the police station, the snow had already stopped and daylight was rapidly fading away. Manhattan, even with its flaws, is such a beautiful city. But when it snows, that layer of freshly fallen snow transforms the city into something magical. Snow can have such a purifying quality to it.

My cell phone showed two missed calls from Jamie while I was at the police station. I didn't call her then because I knew she was likely rushing to prepare for her six o'clock live shot. Rather than interrupt her preparations, I figured I would just wait until returning to my apartment before calling her. Besides, I needed time to myself. Before heading back to my apartment though, I briefly stopped by my office several blocks away from the precinct. Even though the workday wasn't quite over yet, I had no intention of sitting back down at that desk of mine. There was way too much on my mind. I gathered my laptop, then stopped by Eileen's office to let her know that I was back and that everything was fine.

She wanted to hear more, but I kinda deflected her questions, careful not to volunteer too much information. She must have sensed something though, as she told me that I could take a sick day the following day if I wanted. I thanked her but was noncommittal to the offer.

With that I departed my office building on Fifth Avenue, and rather than descend to the subterranean labyrinth of the city's subway system, I wanted to remain aboveground for the thirty-minute walk, zigging and zagging between the avenues and streets, all the way back to my apartment on the Upper East Side. A nice walk in the snow seemed like the perfect opportunity to forget the events of the day, at least for a short while.

Even with the convenient distractions of the holiday storefront displays of Manhattan's finest stores, it didn't take long for the gravity of the situation to land on me with a thud. By going to the police station, I had crossed the point of no return. I was the sole witness to a murder and gave the police a very good description of the killer. The danger became unmistakable when the detective transferred the notes about me from his pad into the NYPD's database. That seemed to cement my involvement in the events of the day. I didn't regret going to the police though, it had to be done, but I knew there would be a cost, I just knew it.

28

BEFORE DICK COULD dial Victor's number, the secure line rang. It was Victor.

"Hello, Victor, I was just about to call you. The name of the witness is David Walker." Dick was quick to throw out the name of the witness to give the appearance of cooperating, but Dick only intended to share only what would serve his purpose. "I learned his name before I even had a chance to run the pictures you sent me against our facial recognition database. He's already been to the police and gave a statement. The NYPD already has a good sketch of your guy. So much for your team pulling this off without any witnesses."

"Dick, your people only gave us two days' advance notice for this operation. Given the short notice and what little information we were provided, this was the only play."

Dick had tried to shift the blame to the SVR, but he knew full well that Victor was right. "For what it's worth, Victor, I was also only given two days' notice. It really isn't that big of an issue anyway. Our side knew the risks of carrying out this operation in broad daylight. If it becomes necessary, the FBI can be brought into the loop, and they can take jurisdiction of the case on national-security grounds. That would effectively squash any investigation."

"Dick, New York's finest is the least of our problems. I also learned something. The three of them knew each other before today."

Dick suddenly snapped to attention, sitting perfectly upright in his high-backed leather chair. "What are you talking about? What three?"

"The three: our little traitor Vasili, the Rosenfeld woman, and this Walker guy. The three of them attended the same art exhibit in Saint Petersburg back in 1995, on April fourth, to be exact, a Tuesday. It was the *Hidden Treasures Revealed* exhibit. It showcased some of the artworks that the Soviet trophy brigades seized from German territory during the war. There has been so much controversy surrounding the subject, so we kept track of those who attended. Everyone entering the museum was required to show identification. We wanted to know who was in attendance. The museum is outfitted with a state-of-the-art surveillance system so we have video footage from the day in question. As we speak, my people are going through the archives to pull the video footage from that day to see if the three spoke to one another."

Dick was silent, contemplating what to make of yet another near impossible to coincidence. He finally replied, "He traveled all the way to Saint Petersburg to go to this art exhibit? Did you pull his travel visa application?"

"Yes, it appears he traveled with a group of other students to attend a one-week business program at a local university. It was during that program that the group visited the Hermitage Museum," replied Victor.

"Where did he apply for his visa for travel to Russia?" asked Dick.

"His university applied for visas for the group from the Russian Embassy in DC," responded Victor. "However, David and two other students traveled from Saint Petersburg to London, not Boston like the rest of the group. There's another interesting detail about Walker. When he arrived at Pulkovo International Airport in Saint Petersburg, passport control noted that several months earlier he had visited Israel. You know the Israelis; they're always up to something. Is there any chance they're involved in this? We know the Rosenfelds have worked with the Mossad in the past to help recover some of their artworks. Maybe he's working for the Israelis."

"Victor, the Israelis know better than to get involved in something like this," responded Dick. "I admit, the three of them being at the exhibit on the same day is one helluva coincidence, but if your people aren't able to find proof on those security tapes, then it's only a coincidence."

"Dick, I don't understand why you're giving this Walker the benefit of the doubt. He's a loose end. We can take care of him for you. Nobody will ever know the truth."

"Victor, this isn't someone who we're going to kill because of a coincidence. I'm still convinced that was just a bystander who made the mistake of following the woman. I cross-referenced their names, and there were literally no connections." Dick had no intention of sharing anything about Walker's neighbor nor the coincidence of the account numbers obtained by Nathalie. "Victor, there's nothing in the agency's systems to even hint at these two knowing each other. Walker works in sales for the telecom company Lucent Technologies; he's been there for the past eighteen months. His offices are only a few blocks from the restaurant. Him being in the restaurant was just a coincidence."

"Dick, you can think what you want to think, but there's no way anyone is going to tell me that it was a coincidence that these three were together at the Hermitage Museum on the same day over four years ago and forty-three hundred miles away, and today they are once again all together under the same roof. I'm Russian intelligence, and none of us would ever accept that."

"Victor, I admit it's one helluva coincidence, but that's all it is at this point. If solid evidence surfaces indicating that Walker and the Rosenfeld woman were working together, then that changes everything. But until then, nothing is going to happen to him."

"Dick, we already have the team in place. We can handle this for the agency. It's not a problem."

"Thanks for the offer, Victor. I'll discuss the situation with my people; then I'll be in touch shortly." Dick knew the decision was his to make. The group that had contacted him in the first place about the operation didn't want to be bothered until everything was resolved. It was Dick's responsibility to find a solution that ensured nothing was going to be exposed. Dick knew that Walker needed to be interrogated to know for certain what he knew, but he wasn't quite ready to give the Russians the go-ahead. He needed a little more time to think things through.

"Okay, Mr. CIA, I'll wait for your call."

29

IT WAS ALREADY dark outside when Detective Lorenzo pulled up to the Rosenfeld's art gallery just before four thirty. He found a perfect parking space near the gallery, right in front of a fire hydrant. After turning off the car's ignition, he reached over to the passenger seat and grabbed hold of the NYPD placard and placed it on the dashboard of his unmarked Ford Taurus.

The gallery had a closed sign on the front entrance but he could see the lights were still on. As the detective reached for the buzzer on the door's frame, the door unexpectedly opened, and a woman in her sixties welcomed him inside.

"Hello, I'm Detective Anthony Lorenzo with the NYPD," he said as he simultaneously showed his badge.

"Hello, Detective, Mr. Rosenfeld told me you were coming. When I saw you park in front of the fire hydrant, I thought it must be you." She used her slightly wry smile as a punctuation mark.

"I'm Jessica Simmons. I've been a family friend for as long as I can remember. I came to the gallery after I heard the terrible news. Mr. Rosenfeld is in his back office. Let me take you back there." She led the way through a cluster of paintings, some hanging on the walls and others just stacked on the floor and leaning on the walls. Clearly there wasn't enough wall space to hang everything. In between the paintings, there were statues, none more than five feet tall, and decorative chairs that looked as if they came from the Palace of Versailles.

Ms. Simmons gave the office door two faint knocks, then a barely audible voice called out from the other side, "Come in."

Ms. Simmons opened the door and peered inside. "Claude, Detective Lorenzo is here to see you."

"Thank you, Jessica. Detective, please come in."

Mr. Rosenfeld's eyes were moist and bloodshot. He remained seated as he shook the detective's hand. Claude had a distinguished style that blended well with his European art collection.

"Mr. Rosenfeld, I'm sorry for the loss of your daughter."

"Thank you for coming, Detective. Please sit."

As Detective Lorenzo was lowering himself into the lone chair beside the desk, he noticed a picture on his desk with a very attractive and much younger woman. Not sure how to phrase it, the detective somewhat haltingly asked, "Mr. Rosenfeld, I hope you don't mind me asking, but is the woman in the picture your daughter, Nathalie?"

"Yes, that is Nathalie. The picture was taken at last year's Cancer Society black-tie gala on the Carnival cruise ship, the MS *Paradise*."

"Your daughter is beautiful." With that single picture, the detective came to understand why she caught the witness's attention. There was something about her that stood out, nothing to put a finger on, but it was just everything about her. Something about her made him think of the witness.

The detective's attention returned to Nathalie's father. "You mentioned on the telephone that you thought your daughter was murdered."

"Yes, Detective, I'm certain of it."

"What makes you so sure?" asked the detective as he pulled out his small notepad from his coat pocket.

"Two days ago Nathalie received a phone call from a stranger. She said he was a Russian by the name of Vasili. The Russian claimed to have pictures that proved that the Russian government was in possession of some of our family's art collection that was stolen by the Nazis during World War II. I knew it was too good to be true. I begged Nathalie not to meet the Russian, but as always, she paid no attention to my concerns. My daughter had no appreciation for danger, Detective. She was determined to meet with him."

"Do you know where your daughter planned to meet with this Russian?"

"Yes, the meeting place was at the Au Bon Pain near Rockefeller Plaza." With a slight pause, Claude continued with a more pensive thought. "Detective, I've known for some time that it was only a matter of time before something happened to Nathalie."

"What made you think that?" asked the detective.

"Nathalie was too stubborn for her own good. A lot of secrets came out of World War II that some very powerful people and groups want to be kept secret. The looting that took place is only the tip of the iceberg. In Nathalie's search for our family's artworks, she made enemies with some powerful people. She had a way of uncovering secrets that others wanted to forget. She enjoyed putting people on notice. It was all or nothing for Nathalie, nothing in between, and this is what got her killed, either directly or indirectly. As far as she was concerned, she was going to retrieve every single item the Nazis stole from her grandfather, or she would die trying. She was that committed to the cause. She was that stubborn. It's hard to reason with a person like that."

"Mr. Rosenfeld, a witness has already come forward and given a statement. He saw your daughter receive a package from a man who looked Russian. After she left the restaurant, it was another man who bumped into her, and then within seconds, she collapsed. We have a good description of this second man."

"Detective, I don't doubt your investigative abilities, but I hold little hope that her murder will be solved."

"Mr. Rosenfeld, I promise you that I'm going to do everything in my power to solve this case."

"I have no doubt, but it's not lack of effort that's going to keep this case from being solved."

"I'll be sure to keep you abreast of the investigation, sir," said the detective as he rose from his chair.

"Thank you again for coming by, Detective."

"Once again, Mr. Rosenfeld, I extend my sincerest condolences to you and your family."

30

MY WALK-UP STUDIO apartment was above a restaurant at the northeast corner of Sixty-Third Street and First Avenue. After climbing the twenty or so stairs to the landing, I reached my apartment, which was the first on the left. Even for Manhattan standards, it was a tiny 275 square feet. Just two steps inside the door put me in the center of the studio, within arm's reach of both my bed and kitchen.

I dropped my laptop bag to the side of the dresser, and without removing my overcoat, did a Nestea plunge onto the bed. I was exhausted—mentally exhausted. I closed my eyes and blocked all thought except that of looking out over the open ocean from land. This image invariably has a way of bringing forth such a sense of inner calm and tranquility. It was in this peaceful state that my subconscious connected the dots.

It was an epiphany moment. Nathalie was Jewish; I knew this not only from the Star of David pendant that hung from her neck but also from her surname. The detective mentioned he was going to see her father at the family-owned art gallery. Businesses like this, in which it takes years to acquire significant collections, are not sold off when the owner dies. This is the type of business that stays in a family for generations. Lastly, the man who handed her the package definitely looked Russian. It was only a hunch, but my intuition told me that whatever got her killed reached back to World War II. Perhaps that was what accounted for that sense of purpose I saw in her.

That moment of clarity was shattered by an abrupt twist of the locked doorknob followed by an impatient and rather testy quick succession of knocks on the door.

"Hold your horses, Kaitlyn," I yelled, even though I knew she couldn't hear me. She was only thirteen years old but had perfected the art of using her knuckles for maximum effect. That knock of hers reminded me of the endearingly obnoxious knock of a former boss. Kaitlyn was my neighbor. She and her mother lived in the apartment opposite mine but a little farther down the hallway. When I opened the door, Kaitlyn just walked past me, obviously annoyed at the indignity of having to wait for me to open the door, then plopped herself on the edge of my bed.

Even though Kaitlyn was deaf, we have no difficulty communicating. She wears a hearing aid but for some reason refuses to wear it at home. As long as I'm looking at her while talking, and open my mouth wide while overenunciating my words, she has no problem understanding everything I'm saying. When she spoke, her speech was somewhat of a monotone drone, lacking crispness. When I was in school, I had such difficulties pronouncing my Rs. Kids can be so cruel at times. If mispronouncing an *R* was enough to be called funny talk, I almost didn't want to know what she was going through.

The biggest mistake someone could make with Kaitlyn was to think that because she was deaf, she wasn't quite capturing what was going on. Which couldn't have been farther from the truth because nothing escaped her notice. Whatever she didn't hear was compensated for in her other senses. The field of neuroscience has demonstrated that when a person is missing one or more of his or her five senses, whether it be sight, smell, touch, taste, or hearing, the brain rewires itself to increase the information flow to the other senses. This, along with the fact that she was an old soul, meant that nothing got past her. I liked that about her.

"What's wrong, David?"

"What makes you think something's wrong?"

"I can see it on your face. You're distracted, or something."

"It's been a long day, that's all." I knew eventually I would share the events of the day with her but wanted to wait until her mother was around. "Is your mother home?"

"Yeah, she's cooking dinner; it's almost done. She wanted me to invite you over. If you're going to the gym, she said she can put a plate aside for you."

"I'm not going to the gym tonight."

"Now I know something's wrong. You always go the gym after work."

"Okay, Nancy Drew, you got me. Something did happen today. I'll share what happened with you and your mother over dinner."

"What is it?"

"I'm telling the both of you together. Let's go see your mom."

With that, we stepped out of my apartment, Kaitlyn leading the way, and after no more than five steps down the hallway, we entered her apartment.

"Mom, David is here."

"Hi, Susan, it smells delicious in here."

Susan was several years older than me, but she looked like she was in her midtwenties. She had straight brownish-reddish hair to the middle of her shoulder blades, with deep blue eyes. She stood about five foot four, and soaking wet she probably weighed barely more than a hundred pounds or so. She was attractive in a subtle, artsy way.

Looking back over her shoulder to make eye contact with a warm smile, she replied, "I'm making orecchiette with pesto sauce and chicken."

"Mom, David's going to tell us about something that happened today. He wanted to tell us together."

"You make it sound so intriguing," replied Susan, knowing how Kaitlyn liked to add her own little dramatic effect to the ordinary.

"Something exciting happen today, David?" asked Susan.

For the next hour over dinner, I shared the events of the day with them, from the moment I entered the restaurant to when I departed the police station.

The seriousness of the events was not lost on either of them. The first words out of Kaitlyn's mouth were, "You're in trouble." She said it not as a question but a statement.

"Oh, Kaitlyn," responded her mother, trying to cover up her own concerns so as to not unnecessarily raise any alarms.

"You two are being silly. It all just happened today. There's no way anyone could know where I live so soon." I said this for their benefit only. "You two, there's nothing to worry about; everything is going to be fine," I continued, quickly changing the subject. "Let me help with the dishes."

"Don't worry about the dishes. Kaitlyn will take care of them."

"Okay then, if you don't mind, I'm going to excuse myself and go back to my place." With that I stood and was followed to the door by both of them. Even though Susan and I had never shared an intimate moment, there was always an energy between us, but we never mentioned it; it was just understood. As I said good-night, I gently rubbed Susan's shoulder and slightly grazed her cheek with my finger, and Kaitlyn without saying anything reached for my free hand and gently squeezed. To calm her nerves, I leaned toward Kaitlyn and placed a kiss on her forehead and smiled at both before going across the hallway.

31

LATER THAT EVENING I spoke with Jamie on the telephone. Jamie was a television news reporter in Hartford, which was about a two-hour drive away. We usually spoke on the telephone a few times a day. A recent promotion meant that she now had weekends off, which meant we were able to see each other most weekends.

"Hi, David. Do you miss me?"

"I always miss you, Jamie." That was true even though we had relationship issues. We met under some unusual circumstances while working for her father; then several years later we started dating. "What did you report on today?"

"The usual, another house fire. We had good video on it, so I went with that." In a nutshell, that's why our news media is so weak. "How did your sales meeting go? Did you make the sale?"

"I missed the sales meeting. I had Eileen take care of it for me."

"Why?"

For the third time, I retold the story, from start to finish.

"It was probably money in the envelope?" said Jamie.

"It definitely wasn't money. I can't envision any circumstance under which she would receive an envelope full of cash. She wasn't there for money. It was something else; I'm certain of it."

"I think it's more likely that it was an envelope full of cash and that she was likely robbed. It's probably just a robbery gone bad."

I didn't even bother to respond.

During the brief pause, she took the opportunity to switch topics. "Did you hear back from the United Nations about that position in Kosovo?"

"No, I still haven't heard anything." Just like the other applications I submitted. The UN embodies the worst of government. It's bureaucratic to the point of near paralysis and the level of nepotism and patronage makes Chicago's political machine seem like amateur hour.

"I thought my father's letter would have helped," replied Jamie.

"His letter would have helped were I applying for something with our government, but the UN is a different animal altogether. I think it's time for me to start exploring other ways to get overseas."

"You're running out of options. Maybe it wasn't meant to be," Jamie suggested.

"It was meant to be, and I will make it happen, somehow, someway. That much I can assure you." Part of me knew that getting overseas

wasn't supposed to be easy, which would make it all the more reward-
ing when it did happen.

"Oh, I almost forgot. I need the hundred dollars from you for the
monthly payment into our mutual fund," said Jamie.

"Okay, I'll give it to you when I see you next. Just make sure that
when it gets cashed out that I get my half."

"Why would I do that? I know how to forge your signature. It's
easier for me to do that and keep it all," replied Jamie.

"Very funny," I responded.

"The news is coming up; I want to watch my repackaged report
from the six o'clock news."

"Before you go, let me give you the detective's telephone number. Just so you have it."

"I'm already in bed. I don't feel like getting up to get a pen and
paper," she replied. "Why do I need it anyway?"

"You probably won't need it. I figured, just in case, you would have
it."

"In case of what? You're being ridiculous," said Jamie.

"Okay, never mind. I'm sure you're right," I replied, not believing
my own words.

"David, I just think you're overreacting. There's nothing you need
to worry about."

"If you don't hear from me by seven a.m., just give a quick call," I asked.

"Okay, I need to go. My story's coming on. I'll talk to you in the morning. Love ya."

"Okay, Love ya too. Good night!"

With the lights out in my apartment, I lay in bed watching the eleven o'clock local news on the NBC affiliate. At eleven thirty, without getting out of bed, I stretched across the room to the television that was sitting on the windowsill and switched the station to watch *Late Night with David Letterman*. I'd been a diehard Letterman fan since the days when his show followed Johnny Carson.

After the Letterman show ended at twelve thirty, I switched off the television and, before I knew it, had fallen fast asleep.

32

I WAS STARTLED awake from a sound sleep at 3:03 a.m. My heart was pounding. I wasn't sure if I dreamed it, but I had heard a vehicle stop on the street below and its doors open and close. Silence followed.

As quietly as possible, I slowly sat up in bed. The building's stairs were on the opposite side of the wall against which my bed was positioned. I placed my ear against the wall and listened intently. I could hear the wooden stairs creaking but couldn't hear any accompanying footsteps, only creaking. I've lived in my apartment long enough to know the sounds the stairs make. The rhythm of the creaking was slower than normal, and the stairs seemed to be under heavier than normal weight.

The creaking noise stopped at my door. My door was locked, but in the darkness of the room, I thought I saw the doorknob twist; then I heard the deadbolt click open. Everything then happened so fast. I got one leg onto the floor before the door burst open. Like a flash, three masked men burst into my studio. There was no escape. The three of them easily subdued me, two of whom held me upright by my arms while the third drilled his fist into my stomach.

The two released their grip on me, and I crumbled to the floor, gasping for breath. I immediately tasted blood. They rolled me onto my stomach and duct-taped my wrists behind my back and my ankles together. Then they threw a hood over my head. The hood was absolutely disgusting. The material was rough like burlap and smelled like it had been in the trunk of a vehicle for years. The hood would be all it would take for their plan to unravel.

Dazed and dressed only in flannel pajama bottoms and a T-shirt, I heard these men whispering in a language that sounded like Russian. They carried me out of my apartment down to their waiting van. I was tossed onto the floor between two rows of seats, and one of my abductors sat near me and pressed his foot against my ribs to keep me still. The doors closed and the vehicle sped off, circling around the block. Knowing the neighborhood as I did, I knew the van jumped on FDR Drive, heading south along the East River.

33

KAITLYN, WHOSE BEDROOM was opposite David's on the other side of the stairs, was awoken at 3:05 a.m. It wasn't something she heard but rather the vibrations she felt as a result of the brief struggle between David and the kidnappers.

Sensing something was wrong, Kaitlyn dashed out of bed to the bedroom window overlooking Sixty-Third Street, where she saw a white van parked in front, the sliding side door open and exhaust coming out of the tailpipe. Three men then came hurrying out of the building carrying someone. Kaitlyn knew it was David and watched as they tossed him onto the floor between two rows of seats. Two of the three kidnappers sat in back, and the third jumped into the passenger's seat. Then the van sped off, taking an immediate right onto First Avenue and disappeared out of view.

Kaitlyn screamed for her mother, but it was too late. By the time her mother made it to Kaitlyn's room, the van was long gone.

"Mom, they took David."

"What are you talking about?"

"I saw three men carry David to a van; then it left and turned onto First Avenue." Susan told Kaitlyn to stay put while she went to peer into the hallway. That was when she saw David's door ajar. She haltingly approached David's door and called to him, but there was no response. She then poked her head inside the apartment and saw the blankets strewn about the room and a chair that had been knocked over. Susan ran back to her apartment and dialed 911.

34

VICTOR YURCHENKO, ALONG with two other SVR team members, was waiting for Walker's arrival at an abandoned warehouse in the oceanfront neighborhood of Brighton Beach. The neighborhood was located in the southern part of Brooklyn and was often referred to as Little Russia, given the number of Soviets who emigrated there in the late 1980s and 1990s.

Victor had just received a telephone call from his team members who were responsible for the kidnapping, and they informed him that they were en route to the warehouse and would be there in twenty minutes.

Victor was a pro. The warehouse was little more than the rusted steel skeletal remains of what had been a fish packaging plant decades earlier. In the center of the open space was a table and three chairs. On the table was a small black bag containing syringes and vials of a pharmaceutical drug named sodium pentothal, also known as truth serum. For someone to lie, it requires a higher brain functioning in the cerebral cortex. What the "truth serum" does is sufficiently reduce the functioning in this part of the brain, thus weakening one's ability to lie. The Russians swear by the drug.

A few hours earlier, Victor had the opportunity to practice his interrogation techniques on Vasili, the man who was willing to sell Russia's state secrets. The traitor, whose face was now little more than a bloodied pulp, was in a backroom, barely clinging to life. He wouldn't be alive much longer though. Once Walker arrived, Victor planned on dragging him out of the backroom so he could execute him in front of Walker. The objective was not only to break Walker's resolve but also to remove any hope Walker may have. Walker had to be made to feel that his fate was already sealed.

Victor had much experience in the field of interrogations. During his three-year assignment in Afghanistan, he tortured and interrogated countless captured Afghan fighters and spies. Like most Soviets, Victor had the best of intentions when he arrived in Afghanistan. It didn't take long for that to change after he saw some of the sadistic ways Afghans used to kill captured Soviet soldiers. War has a way of bringing out the darkness in people.

Victor's reputation took on legendary status when he was on assignment in Beirut, Lebanon, in 1985. Within a month of his arrival, he had to deal with the kidnapping of four Soviet diplomats. This was at a time when Hezbollah had been kidnapping Americans and other Westerners and holding them for ransom and weapons. The Soviets on the other hand had good relations with Hezbollah, likely because they shared a common enemy, the United States. However, an offshoot of Hezbollah calling itself the Islamic Liberation Organization (ISO) decided on its own to kidnap the four Soviet diplomats. ISO mistakenly thought that its Soviet hostages could prove as lucrative for it as the Americans proved to be for Hezbollah. ISO announced that it would kill the diplomats one by one every twenty-four hours until either the ransom was payed or there were no more live hostages. After the first twenty-four hours passed, one of the hostages was found dumped in a landfill with a bullet in his head.

The KGB, with Victor Yurchenko in the lead, took bold action. Through his Hezbollah contacts, Victor learned the identity of the leader of this ISO group. Victor then kidnapped the leader's close cousin, cut off his dick and shoved it in his mouth, and then shot him in the head. The body was then dropped at the family home, with a note listing the names of the group's other male family members, along with a statement that said all those on the list would meet the same fate if the Soviet hostages were not released immediately. Less than twelve hours later, the remaining three hostages were released unharmed.

The Soviets hate being blackmailed. Everyone in the field knew this. No matter what the circumstances, trying to blackmail the Soviets is always a bad idea. The Soviets play hard ball.

35

AS I LAY on the floor of the van, the only thing I could think about was breathing. The punch to my stomach took everything out of me. I was struggling to breathe, taking whatever short gasps I could, and all the while blood continued to flow into my mouth. I couldn't think of anything other than getting more air into my lungs. After a few minutes of this, something else started happening.

The filthy and gasoline-smelling hood that was over my head was causing my skin to have an allergic reaction. I could feel hives breaking out all over my body. I tried to say something, but the kidnapper pressed his foot against my chest as to prevent me from speaking. It started with a tingling on my ears, then turned to a raging itch that spread across my entire body. It felt like I was being eaten alive by ants. I tried squirming to get the kidnapper's attention, but all he did was thrust his foot harder into my chest.

I could feel my airways constricting, and I couldn't breathe. My arms and legs were tied with duct tape, and a foot pressed against my chest; there was nothing I could do. There was no more fight in my body, and I just faded out of consciousness.

36

AS MUCH AS Dick Worthington was determined to protect David Walker, he still knew that David had to be interrogated so that he could know for certain whether Nathalie and David were working together. Dick would have preferred interrogating Walker himself, but once again, it was too risky for the CIA to be directly involved in an operation targeting an American on US soil. Given the fact that the SVR already had a team in place, it made sense for Dick to have the Russians kidnap and interrogate Walker.

However, Dick gave Victor one nonnegotiable condition: unless ironclad evidence surfaced proving David's complicity with the Rosenfeld woman, he was to be released alive within twelve hours of being kidnapped. Knowing full well Victor's reputation as an inter-rogator, Dick went out of his way with Victor to make it clear that if Walker somehow ended up dead, even if by accident, the entire SVR team would be held accountable. Victor had no choice but to accept the terms.

37

IT WASN'T UNTIL the white van reached the warehouse that the kidnappers realized something was wrong. When the hood was removed, the horror beneath was revealed. Without being told what to do, the kidnapper whose foot had been pressed against Walker's chest pulled David out of the van by his ankles and then slung his lifeless body over his shoulder and rushed inside and placed him on the cold concrete floor.

The SVR team froze in disbelief at the sight of Walker's seemingly lifeless body on the concrete floor. The witness's face was distorted by the hives that broke out across his entire body. Walker was unrecognizable from the witness they saw at Au Bon Pain the previous day.

As accusations of incompetence were hurled about, Natasha, the only woman on the team, who was a trained nurse from her previous life, rushed to David's side. Using a knife that materialized from somewhere unseen on her person, she cut the duct tape from David's wrists and ankles, laid him flat, and then put her ear to his chest. He wasn't breathing, but she was able to detect the faintest of pulses on his wrist.

"Is he alive?" asked Victor.

"Barely, but he won't be for long if we don't get him to a hospital," replied Natasha.

"What's wrong with him?" asked Victor.

"He's having an allergic reaction or an asthma attack or something. His airways are swollen shut, and he can't breathe."

"What is it with Americans and fucking allergies?" responded Victor.

"We don't have anything to help him," said Natasha. I'm not trained for this."

Victor yelled, "You better figure something out or we're all going to be in serious trouble!"

"He needs to go to the hospital. There's nothing I can do here."

At that instant it occurred to Natasha that the black medical bag on the table also contained a vial of epinephrine, which is the pharmaceutical name for adrenaline. Adrenaline has many purposes, but in the context of particularly brutal interrogations, the drug is commonly used to keep a person alive long enough to finish the interrogation. What Natasha remembered was that epinephrine was also the active drug contained in EpiPens, which are used to treat severe allergic reactions. The shot helps to relax the muscles that have tightened around the airways during an asthma attack, allowing the airways to open and permitting more air into the lungs, enabling the patient to breathe easier. The drug also relieves severe itching, hives, and other allergy symptoms.

"Get me the black bag on the table," Natasha yelled to no one in particular. The kidnapper whose foot was pressed against Walker's chest during the ride, the one with the most to lose, was the one who moved the fastest to retrieve that bag from the table. He handed her the bag, and she removed the epinephrine and syringe and pushed the needle into the vial to extract a dose of the medicine and without pause injected the needle into David's upper thigh.

Adrenaline shots are fast acting, and within twenty seconds she could see Walker's chest rise and fall ever so slightly. She reached for his wrist to check his pulse, and that was when Walker's hand moved. He blindly reached for Natasha's hand. Hesitating at first, she instinctively took his hand and gently squeezed. A single tear rolled down the side of his face. She gently squeezed his hand again, and this time she felt him trying to squeeze back, and a few more tears trickled down the side of his face. She felt guilty for the role she played. She was the youngest of the group and hadn't yet hardened to the degree of her colleagues. She questioned whether she was even cut out for this work.

Natasha leaned close to David's ear and whispered, "You're going to be okay."

She knew when she saw him in the restaurant that he and the Rosenfeld woman didn't know each other. It was a matter of being in the wrong place at the wrong time. Natasha no longer wanted anything to do with the operation. She certainly didn't save David's life only for him to be interrogated by Victor.

Knowing what needed to be done, she turned directly to Victor with a look of dire urgency. "He's going to die if we don't get him to a hospital."

"What are you talking about? He's doing better now, thanks to you," replied Victor.

"Victor, the shot is temporary. He will die if we don't take him to a hospital for medical treatment," said Natasha, deliberately exaggerating the situation.

"We can't interrogate him?" asked Victor.

"Victor, what aren't you hearing? If he doesn't get to a hospital, he's going to die. It's that simple," said Natasha, in a tone she had never used with Victor. He could feel her concern.

"I can't believe after all this effort we can't even interrogate him because of his allergies!" After a long pause, Victor squatted by Walker's side. "Mr. Walker, today you are a very lucky man. You are lucky, and I am very unlucky."

"Take him to the hospital," Victor instructed the four who kidnapped Walker. "Take him back across the river and drop him at Mount Sinai. Drop him around the corner from the emergency-room entrance so no one sees you, and then come back."

What an opportunity lost, Victor thought. He had been looking forward to having the man with ice-cold blue eyes kill the archivist in front of Walker for dramatic effect; however, Walker's allergies changed everything. Victor looked to the man with the ice-cold blue eyes and reminded him that the traitor in the back room still needed to be dealt with. Without even a second thought, the man who was responsible for taking the life of Nathalie Rosenfeld the day prior matter-of-factly walked to the back of the warehouse, entered the backroom, and fired three gunshots in rapid succession, two to the chest and one to the head.

38

WITHIN TEN MINUTES of Susan's call to 911, the apartment block was swarming with NYPD cruisers. The 911 operator, having confirmed what the caller had said about the kidnapping victim being a witness to suspicious death the day before, immediately called the detective of record to inform him of the development.

The detective was woken at 3:18 a.m. The instant he learned the news, he knew that he had fucked up. He had disregarded Walker's concerns, and now he was kidnapped. Before getting out of bed, he leaned close to his wife to let her know he had to go to a crime scene. She was still sound asleep but still somehow managed to mumble something unintelligible. With that he kissed her on the cheek and then got dressed and headed to Manhattan's Upper East Side.

As the detective drove to the city, he second-guessed himself about how he had treated the witness the day before. The detective reluctantly recalled how the witness had questioned him about putting his name into the NYPD database. The detective thought he was being paranoid about the whole thing. The gravity of the situation was finally sinking in. He knew that whoever learned the witness's identity did so from the NYPD database, which he knew pushed all entries to the FBI's National Crime Information Center (NCIC) data-base. At that point, it's anyone's guess who has access.

How did he fuck up again? he thought. Seven years earlier when he was a patrolman, he and his partner had responded to a domestic disturbance. When he knocked on the door, the couple answered the door together. They explained that the call was a total misunderstand-ing, and he believed them. Within an hour there was another call for a disturbance at the same address. When he and his partner returned to the scene, they found the woman lying in a pool of blood in the living room. She had been stabbed to death. The boyfriend was still in the apartment and confessed to the crime. He was in shock himself. This has always haunted the detective. If he had asked different questions or separated the two for questioning, then maybe it could have been avoided. Did she try to communicate something with her body or facial language that maybe he missed? Whatever the case was, whether or not it was even his fault, her killing weighed on his conscience. He and his partner missed something that day, and now once again he missed something else that could very well cost another life.

Detective Lorenzo was still on the Long Island Expressway (LIE), nearing the Queens Midtown Tunnel into Manhattan when he received a telephone call from the crime scene.

"Hello, Sergeant, I'm on my way. I should be there in another fif-teen minutes."

"Okay, Detective, I wanted to give you a heads up that the feds just arrived to the crime scene."

"Okay, I guess it was only a matter of time before the FBI got involved. Whatever you do, don't let the FBI in Walker's apartment. I'll deal with them when I arrive."

"Okay, Detective, but only one of them is FBI. The other is CIA," replied the sergeant.

"You gotta be kidding me," replied the detective, knowing that this was a game changer.

"Okay, Sergeant, thanks for the call. I'm nearing the Queens Midtown Tunnel. I'll be there in about ten minutes."

Like most in the NYPD, Detective Lorenzo was suspicious of the feds. The department's mistrust of the FBI mostly centered on the fact that while local law enforcement was trying to build their own cases against some of New York's most notorious organized crime figures, the FBI was secretly dealing with these figures, in some cases granting them immunity in return for serving as informants. These organized crime figures then used their relationship with the FBI to their advantage against their rivals. As would be imagined, the FBI running their own operations behind the back of the NYPD caused great mistrust between the organizations.

As for the NYPD's mistrust of the CIA, it had everything to do with the TWA Flight 800 crash investigation. On July 17, 1996, TWA Flight 800 took off from JFK Airport heading to Rome with a stopover in Paris. However, twelve minutes after takeoff, the plane crashed off the coast of Long Island, killing all 230 people onboard.

Over fifty credible eyewitnesses came forward from Long Island who all swore they saw a missile fired from the Atlantic Ocean ascending toward the aircraft moments before it exploded. The NYPD took witness statements from all of them. Normally this would be a joint investigation between the National Transportation Safety Board (NTSB) and the FBI, with the NTSB in the lead, but because international terrorism was suspected, the CIA was brought in to be the lead agency of the investigation, and the NTSB and FBI played support roles.

Insiders knew that the involvement of the CIA signaled a cover-up in the making. The CIA is not even an investigative body but a spy agency. There's nothing transparent in the nature of any spy agency. After all, a spy agency's own survival depends on its ability to weave a web of lies so thick that nobody can ever learn its true motives or intentions.

The CIA then dismissed all the eyewitness accounts and came up with their own version of events. The CIA explained that what the witnesses actually saw was a trail of burning fuel coming from the aircraft falling to the ocean, not a missile heading toward the aircraft. The CIA attributed the confusion to an optical illusion that only made it look like a missile had been fired at the aircraft. The NTSB and FBI both stood behind the CIA's version of events. Later the NTSB would come out with its own report that determined the most probable cause of the TWA 800 crash was the result of a short circuit in the aircraft's center wing fuel tank that ignited fuel vapors, causing the explosion.

The mainstream media then reported the official version of events that explained that the plane exploded due to an internal explosion in its center fuel tank. The media then dubbed any alternative explanations, particularly the missile version, as "conspiracy theories." The easiest way for the media or someone in authority to discredit any opinion that differs from the official version is by labeling it a conspiracy theory. The American population had been conditioned to believe that conspiracy theorists are people who are in the fray, paranoid, unhinged, mentally unstable, and any other negative connotations, when in fact it's just someone who holds an opinion at odds with the official version of events. There was a time when a person like this would be called an "independent thinker," but now they're derisively labeled "conspiracy theorists."

Though it was never reported by the media, the whispers through-out the intelligence community placed blame on Iran for the shoot down of TWA Flight 800 as retaliation for the USS *Vincennes* shoot down of passenger airliner Iran Air Flight 655 on July 3, 1988. The regularly scheduled passenger jetliner was flying from Tehran to Dubai when it was shot down by the USS *Vincennes*, which fired two surface-to-air missiles at the aircraft, killing all 290 passengers. The airliner was shot down while it was still in Iranian airspace and over Iran's territorial waters in the Persian Gulf.

The NYPD knew it was a cover-up of mammoth proportions, but there was nothing they could do about it. Now Detective Lorenzo had both the FBI and CIA at the crime scene. It turned out Walker was entirely justified to be concerned about having his personal informa-tion entered into the NYPD's database.

39

DETECTIVE LORENZO ARRIVED at the crime scene in his Taurus by 4:00 a.m. Amid the throng of police cars and police officers gathered outside the victim's address, there were two men in suits who stood out from everyone else. He knew they were the feds; they had the look.

As soon as the detective stepped out of his vehicle, the sergeant with whom he spoke to on the telephone approached. "Hello, Detective."

"Good morning, Sergeant. Seems like we got quite a circus here. What do we know so far?"

"A few minutes after three o'clock, three men in masks entered the apartment building and then David Walker's apartment. There were no signs of forced entry at either door. Once inside the victim's apartment, there was a brief struggle to subdue him. They then carried him downstairs to a waiting van and sped off, heading north on First Avenue."

"Has forensics arrived yet?"

"Yes, they're in the victim's apartment now. They shouldn't take too long. The studio apartment is tiny."

"Were there any witnesses?" asked the detective.

"Yes, you're gonna love this. The only witness is his thirteen-year-old neighbor named Kaitlyn, and she's deaf. Here's irony for you. Of the eighteen apartments in this six-story walk-up, the only person who knew anything was happening was the single deaf person. Apparently she was awoken by faint vibrations from the floor, probably caused by a brief struggle, and then she went to her bedroom window." The officer pointed to the window. "It's the window one floor up to the right of the entrance. That was when she saw the three men carry the victim out of the building to the van. The victim had a hood over his head, and she said his wrists were tied behind his back, and his ankles were also tied together. They tossed him between two rows of seats in the back, then jumped into the van and took off, heading north on First Avenue."

"Who called nine-one-one?" asked the detective.

"It was the girl's mother, Susan. They're still awake and pretty shaken up. They know the victim well. They're in apartment number two, across the hall from the victim's apartment," replied the officer. "I almost forgot. The girl got a partial plate number."

"You're kidding me," replied the detective.

"Here it is." The officer handed the detective a scrap of paper. "She got the first four digits, but she missed the last three New York tags."

"Have you told the feds anything?" asked the detective.

"Detective, this is an NYPD investigation. I told them nothing."

The detective gave a small, satisfied smile. "After I go upstairs, tell them that I will talk to them when I come back down."

"Will do, Detective."

As Detective Lorenzo approached the entrance, he noticed a powder residue used to lift fingerprints on the lock and door handle. He observed the door carefully and confirmed what the officers had told him: there was no sign of forced entry. The detective headed up the flight of stairs and stopped outside the open door to Walker's apartment and noted once again there were no signs of forced entry. It's unlikely the kidnappers had keys, so he surmised that it was likely they picked the locks, which means they were professionals.

Without stepping inside the apartment, the detective peered into the studio to let forensics know he was there. "Hello, guys."

The two-person team briefly acknowledged the detective's arrival, but they remained focused on the delicate process of lifting prints from the crime scene.

"Have you found anything interesting?" asked the detective.

"There's not much, Detective. No signs of forced entry downstairs or on the apartment door. We looked at the keyholes under a magnifying glass, and there were fresh scratches, indicating the locks were picked. There was a brief struggle from the bed and then to the floor. In the apartment we've only lifted two sets of prints, but they're not likely those of the kidnappers."

"Why do you say that?"

"Both sets can be found throughout the apartment, which means they're from someone who has spent time here. The kidnappers likely came in fast and left even faster. The initial report said the assailants wore ski masks. Given that, it's likely they could have also worn gloves, which is why we're not finding any of their prints."

"Okay, I'll let you guys finish up here. I'm going across the hall to talk with the witness. I'll come back when I'm done."

The detective went across the hallway to apartment number two and knocked on the door. Susan answered the door, with Kaitlyn by her side. The detective showed his badge and introduced himself. Susan invited him into the apartment.

"You must be Kaitlyn," the detective said. He could see that she had been crying. "The police officer downstairs told me you were a very good witness."

Kaitlyn stayed close by her mother's side, without saying anything. As the detective turned toward Susan to speak, Kaitlyn finally spoke. "Is David going to be okay?"

"Kaitlyn, we are going to find him. I promise."

"Detective, David told us how he witnessed a murder yesterday. This kidnapping must be connected, right?" asked Susan.

"It's not possible to say at this time, but it seems probable," replied the detective.

"Kaitlyn, even though you already told the other police officer earlier, do you think you could repeat for me everything you saw?"

Kaitlyn seemed a little reluctant but then nodded in agreement, and told the detective everything.

"Thank you so much, Kaitlyn. If it wasn't for you, none of us would even know that David was missing. I promise you that I'm going to do everything possible to find him." The detective turned to her mother and pulled out one of his business cards and wrote his cell phone number on the back. As he extended his hand to give it to Susan, Kaitlyn gently took the card. She studied it. Susan looked down at her daughter, without saying anything, and ran her fingers through her daughter's hair.

Before leaving, the detective took down Susan's telephone number. "I'll call immediately when I know something," he said, and with that the detective excused himself.

The forensics team hadn't learned anything new, so the detective went back downstairs to talk to the feds. The detective knew they were involved in this mess somehow but didn't know how. Until he could figure out the how, he had to behave himself because he knew they could take jurisdiction of the investigation and cut him entirely out of the loop. The detective knew the only way he could help Walker was to remain on the case for as long as possible.

As much as the detective was trying to play nice, when they introduced themselves to one another, he couldn't help asking them in his sarcastic tone, "Are you guys on the feds' rapid-response team?"

"I'm not sure I follow," said the FBI special agent.

"I was surprised to see you guys here so fast. If you don't mind me asking, how did you guys learn about the kidnapping?"

Because the FBI special agent was just brought in at the last minute, Dick Worthington did all the talking. "For reasons that can't be disclosed, this Nathalie Rosenfeld was on the CIA's watch list. Therefore, when you created a database entry for her, the update was automatically sent to the National Crime Information Center's (NCIC) database, which then pushed the information to my agency's computers, and that's how I learned about the Rosenfeld woman's death. Because this David Walker was listed in the Rosenfeld entry as a witness, we also received the update about him when the kidnapping was called in." Dick was satisfied with his own response, knowing he presented an airtight scenario that made sense.

Even though the explanation made sense, Detective Lorenzo didn't trust a word the CIA guy said. Before they could continue, Dick's cell phone rang. A discreet look at the screen told Dick it was Victor. He excused himself before walking across the street to answer the call. The Detective was curious who was calling Dick at four thirty in the morning. Dick returned a few minutes later and suggested that they regroup at the precinct later that morning. The feds departed the scene in the same car, with the spook behind the wheel. The detective knew they were up to something, but he could only wonder.

It was when the detective was heading back upstairs to follow up with the forensics team that he received the telephone call informing him of the news that Walker had been dropped at Mount Sinai Hospital's ER. He was being treated for an asthma attack, but he was in stable condition. That was all the detective knew, but it was enough to know he was off the hook for Walker.

Before leaving the scene to head to the hospital, he informed the forensics team of the update and asked them not to take any of the victim's personal effects to the police station and book them into evidence. "Leave everything in the apartment," he instructed them. The reason for this was twofold. He knew the feds being involved meant it was only a matter of time before they took over jurisdiction of the case. The move was to make sure they didn't take possession of any evidence. Second, he knew Walker would need these things when he got discharged.

"Do you guys have his apartment keys and cell phone?" asked the detective.

"Right here, Detective," one of them said, holding up an evidence bag containing both.

"Great; I'm taking those to the victim at the hospital. How much longer will you guys be?"

"We're pretty much done. Maybe a few more minutes; then we'll be finished."

"Okay, when you're done, lock the door behind you."

Detective Lorenzo was smiling when Susan and Kaitlyn opened their door. "I've got great news, Kaitlyn. David is okay. He's at the emergency room at Mount Sinai Hospital. He's being treated for an asthma attack. The hospital says he'll be fine."

The news was as much a relief for the detective as it was for Kaitlyn and her mother. Tears rolled down Kaitlyn's cheeks as she hugged her mother.

"Girls, if you don't mind, I need to excuse myself. I have to get to the hospital. The both of you have had a long night; you should try to get some sleep."

"Thank you so much for the terrific news, Detective. What an emotional rollercoaster ride it's been," said Susan.

"You're most welcome, Susan," replied the detective as he walked away.

40

I VAGUELY RECALL being unceremoniously dropped on the slush covered sidewalk wearing only my flannel pajama bottoms and T-shirt. I was freezing. It wasn't lost on me that hours earlier Nathalie's life had ended in such a similar way. As for me, I knew this wasn't to be my end. That window had already opened and closed.

When I was finally discovered outside, I could hear a small commotion around me before being lifted onto a stretcher and rolled into the emergency room. My freezing wet pajamas were quickly cut away. The staff, having witnessed a spike in allergies of epidemic proportions over the past few decades, knew precisely what to do. Within no time my difficulty breathing resolved itself, and the hives disappeared.

It was at this point that I managed to communicate to a nurse my name and explained that I had been kidnapped and asked her to call the police to let them know I was there.

Even though I had only met Detective Lorenzo the day before, it was still nice to see a familiar face when he entered my hospital room.

"Hello, David, you've had quite a busy morning!"

"Yeah, you could say that, but I don't remember too much."

"The doctor told me that you're going to be discharged shortly," said the detective.

"I'm feeling fine now. Earlier I thought I was going to die, but now I'm okay."

"Your neighbors, Susan and Kaitlyn, were very worried about you. Kaitlyn was the one who alerted her mother that you had been kidnapped. In that whole building, Kaitlyn was the only one who heard anything. If it wasn't for her, no one would even know anything happened to you."

"Yeah, she's a special one in so many ways."

"David, I need to apologize to you for yesterday. You voiced your concerns, and I thought that you were overreacting. I'm sorry for that. I know now that this case is bigger than I realized. I should have trusted your instincts. I won't let you down like that again."

"Thank you for saying that, Detective. If I were in your shoes, I would have been skeptical too. When I saw that man hand the envelope to Nathalie yesterday and decided to follow, never in my wildest imagination did I think it would lead to this."

"Are you able to tell me what happened this morning?"

I told the detective everything I could remember, which wasn't much. Three men burst into my apartment a little after three. Two held me upright while the third drilled his fist into my stomach. My wrists and ankles were then taped; then a burlap hood was placed over my head. The hood, I explained, that dirty hood, was what triggered my allergic reaction and asthma attack. After that I struggled to breathe for a short while and then lost consciousness. I also remembered that the men were speaking Russian.

There was one other detail that I didn't share because I wasn't sure whether it was real or imagined. During the ordeal, sometime after losing conscientiousness, the most beautiful Russian-accented English voice whispered to me, "You're going to be okay." The words were spoken in such a calming way. *That voice saved me*, I thought, but I didn't share that anecdote.

"Why do you think the Russians took you to the hospital?" The detective wasn't able to reconcile why the Russians were concerned about David's wellbeing enough to take him to the hospital, but yet they went through the effort of kidnapping him.

"I don't have any idea," I replied as my mind had once again wandered back to Nathalie.

"Detective, can you tell me about the meeting with Nathalie's father?"

"He said that an unknown Russian named Vasili was trying to sell her pictures that would prove that the Russian government was in possession of some of her family's art collection that was stolen by the Nazis during World War II. I'm not sure why the Russians would have the artworks if they were stolen by the Nazis though."

"It actually makes sense, Detective. The Nazis looted everything they could get their hands on during World War II and then shipped it all back to Germany. However, by the end of the war, Germany was occupied by many armies, the Americans, British, and Soviets, among others. The Soviets themselves had suffered so much at the hands of the Nazis that they stole all the looted property and treasures, whatever they could get their hands on, and shipped it all back home. That's how so much of Europe's looted art ended up in the Soviet Union."

"Thanks for the history lesson, David."

"I'm a history guy, Detective. Searching for her family's stolen art-works might explain that sense of purpose I described about her. It must have been very personal for her. I know it would be for me."

"The man you saw in the restaurant who passed the package to Nathalie must have been this Russian."

"Yes, that was definitely him."

"Detective, did you tell her father that I want to meet with him?"

"To be honest, I forgot to mention it."

"Please call him for me this morning if you could. I want to meet with him to pay my respects."

"David, there's something else I need to tell you. You were right about being concerned about my entering your information into the database yesterday."

"How so?"

"At the crime scene this morning, both the FBI and CIA were there. They learned of you as a witness to the Rosenfeld case from the entry I made to the database. First it was the Russians, and now the FBI and CIA are involved. Something is going on, but I don't know what to make of it."

As I was contemplating what everything meant, the detective continued. "You've had a crazy morning. You should get some rest before they discharge you. I need to head to the precinct to follow up on a few things."

What he didn't say was that he was going back to the precinct to review yesterday's surveillance footage from the restaurant and sidewalk area.

"There are two police officers guarding your room now. They will stay with you when you're discharged and will drive you to your apartment." The detective then reached into his coat pocket and removed the evidence bag containing the keys and cell phone, "I thought you would need these when you got out of here." He placed the bag on the bedside table.

"Good thinking. I didn't have time to take them earlier," I said, with a wry smile.

Once the detective left the room, without any pause, my thoughts returned to Nathalie. I had downplayed my interest to the detective in meeting with Nathalie's father. The truth was, I had to meet with him to learn something, anything, about the woman I couldn't stop thinking about.

41

TIME WAS OF the essence when the detective returned to the precinct. He knew it was only a matter of time before the feds claimed jurisdiction of both the Rosenfeld and Walker investigations. Once this happens he would be forced to handover all evidence from both investigations. He recalled how during the TWA 800 crash investigation, the FBI collected all evidence, including all the eye-witness statements from the NYPD.

The computer disks containing the surveillance footage were on Detective Lorenzo's desk when he arrived at the precinct. The footage was from six cameras, two from inside the restaurant and four from cameras located nearby on buildings along Forty-Eighth Street.

Before viewing the video footage, the detective had the presence of mind to make copies of the CDs and to photocopy his notes for both investigations. The duplicate disks and photocopies were then placed inside a miscellaneous file folder inside the filing cabinet off to the side of his desk.

Then, after closing his office door, he viewed the surveillance videos, one after another. By the time he finished watching the surveillance videos, he had more information than he could believe. What he witnessed was a well-choreographed operation unfolding before his very eyes. He watched Walker enter the restaurant and exactly as he said, took notice of the woman, then watched as a man handed off an envelope. He understood for himself what Walker meant when he described how Nathalie Rosenfeld stood out against the crowd. He then watched Walker follow the woman out the door. It was at this point, out of the corner of the screen, he noticed a man and woman hurriedly stand from their table and take up pursuit. While the woman was standing from the table, the detective noted that it appeared she was speaking into the sleeve of her coat.

In the next video, the detective watched the Russian who handed Nathalie the envelope walking along Forty-Eighth Street toward Times Square, where he was intercepted by two men who emerged from a dark-colored 1995 Ford Explorer. The two men, one on each arm, led him to the waiting vehicle. The detective couldn't get a clear read on the vehicle's license plate. Under normal circumstances, he could send the video to the FBI crime lab at Quantico and they could enhance the video, but in this case he knew that was not an option.

Lastly, he watched Nathalie walking on Forty-Eighth Street toward Fifth Avenue, when a man wearing a fedora cut across her path, with his hand raised close to her face. Within about one to two seconds, she collapsed on the sidewalk. The detective was now convinced, as Walker had said yesterday, that this man had killed Nathalie Rosenfeld. Everything happened in plain sight, but it was done in a manner that would have gone completely undetected were it not for Walker's eye-witness account. He then watched the man wearing the fedora retrieve the envelope from her handbag and then disappear out of camera view toward Fifth Avenue. As he continued watching the video clip, he then saw Walker approach the Rosenfeld woman as she lay on the sidewalk. He watched as Walker knelt beside her, removing his glove and touching the front of her coat. The couple who followed from the restaurant were nearby, watching Walker's every move. After Walker left the scene heading toward Rockefeller Center, they followed after him, out of view of the camera.

Detective Lorenzo's instincts told him to watch the street-view videos again. There was something else. He knew that the woman who spoke into her sleeve was likely communicating with someone outside the restaurant. Given the many moving parts to the operation that he had already witnessed, he thought it was likely that there was a surveillance vehicle coordinating the operation. Once he knew what he was looking for, he quickly spotted the white van directly out front of the restaurant. It had tinted windows and no identifying markings, and from where it was parked, it had a perfect view of everything. Sure enough, within two minutes of Nathalie collapsing, without anyone entering or leaving the van, it drove off. Even better, the detective could read the New York license plate. Without even looking at his notepad, he knew the first four numbers matched the ones given to him by Walker's neighbor, Kaitlyn.

This case was taking on a life of its own. The detective wanted to run the plate number but knew that it would only be a matter of time before his query reached the feds, and they would realize that he was slowly connecting the dots. He thought it wise to keep his cards close to his chest for the time being.

42

AFTER BEING DISCHARGED from the hospital, the two patrol-men drove me back to my apartment. One of the officers insisted on taking a look inside the apartment before allowing me to enter. Once everything checked out, he went back downstairs to wait. The plan was for me to shower, and then the police would take me back to the precinct to meet with Detective Lorenzo.

As I stood in the middle of the studio, it was surreal to think that only a few hours earlier three Russians had burst into my apartment and kidnapped me. The fact that the Russians' plans were thwarted by my allergic reaction brought a smirk of pride to my face. Satisfied with how things played out, I removed the scrubs given to me by the nurse to wear home and jumped in the shower.

As much as I tried to clear my head, my thoughts, like a compass finding due north, went back to Nathalie. Even after her death and my surviving the kidnapping, the feeling of being drawn to her was stronger than ever. I was convinced that I was meant to see her at Au Bon Pain. It was almost as if the events of the previous day, from noticing her to being the sole witness to her murder, had been a forgone conclusion. I knew there was more though. I just knew there was something waiting to be discovered.

By the time I got dressed, it was 7:30 a.m., and I still hadn't heard from Jamie. As much as I wanted to let her know about the kidnapping, another part of me refused to call her. I had specifically told her to call me if she hadn't heard from me by seven. I was being too stubborn for my own good, but it bothered me that she hadn't called to make sure everything was okay.

Rather than expend any more thought on Jamie, I walked to the apartment across the hallway, where I knew there were two people waiting to hear from me. Susan opened the door, and before I could say anything, she took me by the hand and pulled me inside, shutting the door behind me with her free hand. Without saying anything, she tightly wrapped her arms around me. We stood in a tight embrace, without speaking a word, cheek to cheek, chest to chest, pelvis to pelvis. I could feel the beating of her heart. After maybe thirty seconds of silence, she raised her hand to touch the side of my face. Though we had never shared a romantic encounter, it always felt like it was only a matter of time before it happened. My right hand slowly made its way up her back to gently massage the back of her neck with my thumb while my fingers massaged the lower part of the back of her head.

Without any words, our heads turned toward one another, and our lips came together for a much-anticipated and long-overdue kiss. It was absolutely amazing. The kiss started slow, deep, and passionate, and the longer we kissed, the more intense and ravenous it became. Neither of us showed any signs of wanting the kiss to end, ever. I've never understood the people who say a kiss is just a kiss.

What made the kiss even better was knowing that we weren't going to move beyond the kiss because Kaitlyn was in her bedroom sleeping. As much as we wanted more, we instead channeled all of that desire into the kiss itself. It was a kiss like no other, and it made me feel entirely alive, which was what I needed after the events of the morning.

The kiss gave my heart such a warm, alive feeling. Our mouths parted, and I angled my head slightly to the side so I could kiss her neck while my hands roamed across her shoulders, back to her lower neck, then down her arms to her hands, then interlocked my fingers with hers. Gently, I moved her hands to the small of her back and held them there with one hand as my now free hand slowly caressed up her arm to her shoulder, then down to the outside of her small yet firm breast, and then along her taut ribcage. The kissing went from her mouth, neck, cheekbones, and then back to her mouth. We couldn't get enough of each other, and it was at this point that I took a small step back, putting some distance between us.

We looked into each other's eyes with a sheepish fraction of a smile on our faces.

"I wish we could do that all day long, but I need to get going. The police are downstairs waiting to take me to the precinct."

"I understand. Do you want to come by for dinner tonight?"

"Yes, that would be terrific. Can I say a quick hello to Kaitlyn before I leave?"

"Of course, she'd be furious with me if she knew you came by, and I didn't wake her. Come on; we'll surprise her."

We walked in Kaitlyn's bedroom, and I sat on the edge of her bed. She was facing away from me as I stroked her hair. When she turned and opened her eyes and realized it was me, she immediately sat up and wrapped her arms around me.

With a little sniffle, Kaitlyn said, "I knew you were going to be okay. I just knew it."

"The police detective told me you were the only person in the entire building who was awoken by the kidnappers."

Kaitlyn didn't respond but gave a small nod.

"Thank you so much, Kaitlyn. You are so special."

"I need to go to the police station now, but maybe I'll see you tonight." I then leaned forward and give her a kiss on her forehead.

Susan walked me to out to the door. I took her by the hand, gently taking hold of her fingers.

"I'll see you tonight," said Susan. "Don't let anything happen to you; I want to see you tonight. I'm going to try to bribe Kaitlyn to see if maybe she could spend the night at a friend's, hopefully."

"Okay, I'll see you tonight." And we kissed good-bye.

43

BEFORE DOING ANYTHING else, the detective placed a call to the ME's office for any updates and to confirm that the necessary tests were to be given priority. Even though it was still early, there was always someone at the ME's office.

"Good morning, this is Detective Lorenzo with the NYPD."

"Good morning, Detective. How can I help you?"

"Is Dr. Carlisle available? I'm following up on the preliminary results of an autopsy that he was going to perform yesterday."

"Dr. Carlisle is not in right now, but I should be able to help you. What is the name of the decedent?"

"The name is Nathalie Rosenfeld."

"Detective, the autopsy was never performed. In fact, I don't think the body ever arrived."

"I called yesterday and spoke with Dr. Carlisle. He confirmed for me that the ME had sent a vehicle to transport the victim from the hospital to the ME's office so an autopsy could be performed and toxicology tests could be completed."

"Detective, I don't know what to tell you, but the body never arrived. There are notes in the system. Apparently, the body was taken for cremation. The notes say that she died of natural causes and that her body was cremated as per the family's request."

"You gotta be kidding me. This was a homicide investigation, and now you're telling me the victim's body was cremated? I'll be in touch, but you better figure out how this happened because someone's going to lose his or her job over this."

As irate as the detective was, once he calmed down, he knew that this mishap had nothing to do with the ME's office but bore the hallmarks of the work of the CIA.

44

THAT MORNING, THE NYPD commissioner received a telephone call from the FBI assistant director from FBI Headquarters in Washington, DC, informing him that the FBI, on national-security grounds, was claiming jurisdiction of the Nathalie Rosenfeld death investigation, along with the subsequent Walker kidnapping investigation.

The commissioner, without hesitation, offered the NYPD's fullest cooperation. The commissioner then called the captain in charge of the Eighteenth Precinct, Detective Lorenzo's boss, to inform him that the FBI would be taking over jurisdiction of the investigations and that he expected full-cooperation with the FBI.

Detective Lorenzo was in his office when his desk phone rang. A quick glance at the telephone's digital display told him that it was the captain calling, and he had a good idea about what.

"Hello, Captain."

"Detective, come to my office. We need to talk."

"Okay, Captain, I'll be right over."

The captain knew the news was going to upset the detective, so he started the conversation with some small talk before delving into the matter at hand.

"I heard you had an early morning, Detective," the Captain said.

"As I'm sure you heard, the witness to the Rosenfeld investigation was briefly kidnapped this morning. It appears the plans went awry when the witness had a serious asthma attack. It seems the kidnappers decided to drop him at the hospital. The case is getting even more bizarre. I learned this morning that the Rosenfeld woman was cremated instead of being sent to the ME's office for an autopsy and toxicology testing. Captain, there's more than meets the eye with this case. This witness seems to have stumbled upon something."

"Detective, let me stop you there. Someone from FBI headquarters spoke to the commissioner early this morning. The reason I called you into my office was to inform you the Rosenfeld and Walker cases have been transferred to the FBI on national-security grounds. An FBI special agent will be here shortly to pick up the files, witness statement, and any other evidence related to the cases."

Detective Lorenzo protested the decision, but the captain made it clear that the decision was final and not open to discussion. The detective was told in direct terms that he was to cease any and all work on those investigations.

45

WHEN I ARRIVED at the precinct, the detective led me to an interview room so we could have a private conversation. He informed me that the FBI was on its way to the precinct and had taken jurisdiction of Nathalie's murder investigation and my kidnapping on national-security grounds.

The detective went on to tell me about all he had learned since we last saw each other at the hospital. It turns out the security tapes revealed that no less than eight people had the handoff under surveillance, one of whom was a woman. After the handoff, two of the eight intercepted the man who handed the envelope to Nathalie as he approached Times Square and drove him away in a Ford Explorer. He also shared how he saw on the video how the man wearing the fedora deliberately collided with Nathalie, with his left hand raised, and how seconds later Nathalie collapsed to the sidewalk.

He also mentioned that Nathalie's remains had somehow been mistakenly cremated, which meant there would be no autopsy or toxicology testing. For this to have happened, he confided that it was likely that somehow, either directly or indirectly, the FBI and CIA were involved.

"Detective, what about Nathalie? Have you learned anything else about her?"

"Nothing. I told you everything I know at the hospital," replied the detective. "I almost forgot. I called Natalie's father for you this morning. You were right; he wants to meet with you."

"Did he mention a time?"

"The patrolmen can drive you to his home on Fifth Avenue when we're done here." The detective wrote the father's name and contact information on a page from his notebook and then tore it out and handed it to me. The detective didn't even suspect that I had ulterior motives in meeting with Nathalie's father.

"Thanks for this, Detective. I truly appreciate you setting this up for me."

It was when we stood to end our meeting that the detective took notice of the gloves in my hand. "Are those the gloves you wore yesterday?" asked the detective.

"Yes, why?"

"In the tapes, you knelt beside her and took off your glove, the right glove I believe, and rubbed the front of her coat. Right?"

"Yeah, I think so," I replied.

"You then put your glove back on, right?"

"Yes."

The detective knew that Locard's Exchange Principle in the field of forensics says that any contact between two individuals or objects will leave evidence of some sort that resulted from the two surfaces coming into contact with one another.

"It's quite possible that there was residue of some sort on the front of her coat from whatever was used to kill her. When you touched her coat, it must have gotten on your hand. You then put your hand back into your glove. There should be residue from whatever killed her inside your glove. That glove is the last chance there is of learning what killed her."

"You can have the glove," I told him as I handed it over.

"I'm going to have it tested," said the detective. "Don't mention anything to the feds about the glove. I don't want to give them a heads up."

"Don't worry, Detective. I'm not trusting anyone but you."

"I need to get back to my desk before the feds arrive."

"I'm sure they're going to ask about your whereabouts. I'll tell them you're in protective custody. If they push the issue, you may have to sit with them later."

"Okay, I'll be in touch after I meet with the father."

"I'll see you later," replied the detective.

46

IT WASN'T UNTIL Jamie was leaving for work that morning that she realized she hadn't heard from David. Not wanting to be late, she figured she would call when she arrived at work. When she arrived at work, she found her colleagues already assembled for the morning meeting, so she joined them without making the call.

Jamie finally got out of her meeting at 9:30 a.m. and then tried to call David on his cell phone, but her call went to voice mail. She was wishing that she had taken down the numbers David wanted to give her.

47

MR. ROSENFELD LIVED in one of the most exclusive residential buildings on Fifth Avenue, directly across from Central Park. A doorman waiting dutifully under the canopy out front opened the door for me as I approached the entrance. Once inside the renaissance-style lobby made from Italian marble, I introduced myself to the concierge sitting behind the desk.

"Hello, Mr. Walker. Mr. Rosenfeld told us to expect your arrival," said the concierge. He escorted me into the elevator on the other side of the foyer and stepped in behind me, and with elevator key in hand, he unlocked the button for the penthouse on the eighth floor and then stepped out of the elevator for me to make the ascent alone.

By the time the elevator doors opened, standing in the open door to the residence was a distinguished-looking man who looked to be in his sixties. I was glad I made the right choice that morning while getting dressed to wear my nicest suit.

"Hello, David, I'm Claude Rosenfeld, Nathalie's father."

"Hello, Mr. Rosenfeld. I want to express my sincere condolences for the loss of your daughter, Nathalie."

"Please call me Claude, and thank you for coming by," he said, gesturing for me to come inside. Family and friends had already started arriving, so he escorted me to the study, where we could have some privacy. Once inside the study, Nathalie's father motioned with his hand for me to sit in a large leather chair opposite from the one he was lowering himself into.

"Where are you from?" asked Mr. Rosenfeld. "That's an interesting accent you have."

"I'm from Rhode Island, but to be honest, people there also think I have an accent. Here in New York people think it's a Boston accent, in Boston they think it's a Brooklyn accent, and in Rhode Island they just think I'm from somewhere else. It's always been like that."

I could sense that Nathalie's father was trying to gauge me.

"What do you do for a living, David?"

"I'm a sales representative for Lucent Technologies in Midtown, near where I saw Nathalie yesterday at Au Bon Pain," I replied. I could tell that my mentioning of Nathalie was premature. It was clear he wanted to continue with his questioning before we discussed his daughter.

"Lucent is a good company," replied her father.

"It's okay, but I don't like my job," I replied.

"What is it you don't like about it?" asked Mr. Rosenfeld.

"I'm not a sales guy. It doesn't suit me," I replied.

"Then why don't you find a job that is suitable?" replied Mr. Rosenfeld.

"That's a very good question, Mr. Rosenfeld. To make a long story short, I've been trying to head overseas for a different kind of experience, but it's proven to be more difficult to make happen than I expected. That's why I ended up at Lucent," I explained.

"If that's what you really want, then you need to make it happen," said Claude.

"I agree. I haven't given up. I'll make it happen eventually. Who knows? Maybe I'll join the Peace Corps," I replied, with a quick lift of an eyebrow.

"That sounds like a good idea," replied Nathalie's father. "That would certainly qualify as a 'different kind of experience.' The journey of a thousand miles begins with one step."

"I believe it was Lao Tzu who said that."

"You're a reader," said Mr. Rosenfeld, as more of a statement than a question.

"Somewhat. I'm a liberal arts guy at heart, so I'm curious by nature. I read about almost everything. One week it's Che Guevara, and the next week it's the wine industry in the Republic of Georgia. I enjoy learning; that's part of why I want to work overseas. There's no better education than traveling the world and learning about new cultures and peoples."

It was obvious Mr. Rosenfeld was trying to get a read on me. After a long, thoughtful look, he asked, "Detective Lorenzo told me you were adamant about meeting with me. May I ask why?"

"Mr. Rosenfeld, to be completely honest, I haven't been able to stop thinking about Nathalie since the moment I saw her yesterday.

She singularly captured my undivided attention in such an inexplicable way. She was so beautiful and with such presence. It would have been impossible for me not to have noticed her. Anyhow, that's what compelled me to follow her when she departed the restaurant. Then to watch her get killed before my very eyes, and as the sole witness. I just had to meet with you."

"David, I do appreciate that you wanted to speak with me. New York City can be quite an impersonal place, so it means a lot. However, I think for your own safety you're making a mistake coming here. The detective told me what happened to you this morning. It's very likely that the people who kidnapped you were the same ones who killed my daughter. Why they were concerned enough about you to drop you at the hospital, I have no idea. But I assure you, if you start poking around, you will meet the same fate as Nathalie."

"Mr. Rosenfeld, I'm only here to put my mind to rest." I felt slightly guilty for saying that because I wasn't being entirely honest about my intentions. There was a gap of silence, so I used it as an opportunity to continue. "The detective mentioned that Nathalie was at Au Bon Pain yesterday to meet with a Russian who was supposed to give her pictures that proved the Russian government was in possession of your family's artworks that the Nazis had looted."

Mr. Rosenfeld slightly hesitated, but I felt his resolve weakening. "Was it Nathalie who chose to meet at the restaurant?" I asked.

After another pause, Mr. Rosenfeld spoke. "The Russian wanted to meet at his hotel in Times Square, but Nathalie was the one who insisted on meeting at Au Bon Pain. She had convinced herself that the restaurant would be a safe place to meet."

"Do you know what hotel he was staying at?" I asked.

"I believe she said it was the Marriott Hotel in Times Square," he responded. "Why do you ask?"

"No reason; just curious," I replied. "I saw the Russian hand Nathalie an envelope. It must have been the pictures."

Mr. Rosenfeld continued where I left off. "The plan was for him to bring a small sampling of pictures of our family's stolen artworks. She didn't want to sit down with him until she verified that the pictures were authentic. That was the plan."

It occurred to me that if the pictures in the bulging six-by-nine envelope were only a small sampling, then the Russian must have had quite a few pictures in total. It also occurred to me that it would have been unlikely for him to have traveled from Russia with all those pictures in his suitcases or carry-on. It would have been too risky for him passing through airport security in Russia. If those pictures were discovered, he would have been in serious trouble. It was more likely that he traveled to America with only the negatives. This would prove to be another salient detail.

"Mr. Rosenfeld, the detective mentioned that Nathalie was mistakenly cremated." Even though she was dead, I couldn't bring myself to say *Nathalie's remains* or *Nathalie's body*. I just said *Nathalie*.

"It was no mistake. Somebody made it happen to destroy whatever evidence may have remained."

I also knew it was no mistake. In fact, I'd say it was the FBI and CIA guys the detective said were at my apartment this morning who were responsible for the cremation fiasco. What I also knew was that the feds wouldn't be involved to this extent if this was only about looted artworks. There had to be something else.

"Mr. Rosenfeld, when I knelt beside Nathalie on the sidewalk, I noticed she was wearing a Star of David pendant around her neck. It was so beautiful. It looked like it came from another time. Was it a family heirloom?"

"Yes, that pendant has been in my family for many generations. I have it with me now actually," he said as he reached into his inside suit pocket and removed an envelope containing the thin necklace and six-pointed Jewish star pendant. "I had the presence of mind to remove it from her neck at the hospital yesterday."

"Can I take another look at it?" The heaviness of the piece still surprised me. "Platinum?" I asked, but already knew the answer.

"Yes, it is made of platinum that was mined in the Ural Mountains. It belonged to my grandmother, my father's mother. It was my grand-mother's great-great-great-grandfather who made the pendant; he was a jeweler. Most people don't realize anti-Semitism had taken root in Russia long before Hitler. The first pogroms in Russia started in the early nineteenth century. That's why my ancestors fled the region and resettled in France. They mistakenly thought it would be safer for Jews in France. My family emigrated to America only weeks before the German Army occupied France in the spring of 1940. I was only five years old at the time. The family we left behind, grandpar-ents, aunts and uncles, nieces and nephews, were all deported to the concentration camps, where they were all murdered.

"Before my family fled France, my grandmother insisted that my father take that pendant for safekeeping. We weren't allowed to take any valuables with us, so my father sewed that Jewish star into the lining of his overcoat. That was the only valuable he took. That Star of David pendant survived the pogroms in Russia and cheated the Holocaust."

"It's such a beautiful pendant." The Star of David is simply the compound of two equilateral triangles and is one of the most recognizable symbols in the world, associated with Judaism and the state of Israel. "The piece is so simple and yet so elegant," I said as I handed it back. "When I saw the pendant on Nathalie's neck, I just knew it had a history."

"David, you don't have a Jewish name, but are you Jewish by any chance?"

"Not that I know of, but ever since a middle-school trip to see the play *Fiddler on the Roof*, I've had the faint suspicion that maybe in a past life I was a Jew from the early nineteenth century in Odessa. I know how crazy that sounds, but it's the truth. I just realized, I don't think I ever shared that with anyone."

"Odessa? Why Odessa?"

"I don't know. I didn't choose Odessa. Odessa chose me."

"My grandmother's great-great-great-grandfather, the jeweler? He was from Odessa, and that's where he made the pendant. The pogroms in Russia? They started in Odessa in the early 1820s, and that's why he fled with his family.

"Just another coincidence, I guess. Another layer to the intrigue," I said as I gave a slight smile and raised an eyebrow. "Mr. Rosenfeld, is there any way you could tell me a little something about your daughter? I'm just trying to make sense of everything, and it would help if I had a better idea of who she was. If you don't mind, of course."

I wasn't sure how he was going to respond. He had such a distinguished and self-assured presence, but when I asked him to tell me about his daughter, I could see the pain come across his face. As distraught as he was, he confided that he knew it was only a matter of time before something happened to Nathalie. He told me how it had become Nathalie's mission in life to locate all the valuables the Nazis had stolen from her grandfather. She also wanted retribution. She seethed at the thought that there were still Nazis alive, breathing the same air as her. She could never get past that.

Mr. Rosenfeld described Nathalie as having the unwavering resolve of an activist with zero appreciation for the dangers involved. Unlike the rest of her family, she couldn't bring herself to move on. She wanted all Nazis and anyone who profited from them to be held accountable, regardless of how much time had passed. For Nathalie, "It was a matter of principle."

It was this comment about how "it was a matter of principle" that resonated with me. This remark brought me back to a telephone conversation I had with a researcher at the Simon Wiesenthal Center (SWC) some fourteen years earlier. The researcher, questioning my motives for reporting my neighbor whom I suspected of being a Nazi war criminal, asked why I was reporting my neighbor. My response was simple. I told him that if my neighbor was involved with any of the atrocities committed during the war, regardless of how much time had passed, then he should have to account for those crimes. "It was a matter of principle," I told him.

"Mr. Rosenfeld, with all due respect, I don't understand how anyone, let alone any Jewish person, could ever bring him- or herself to forgive the Nazis for what they did. It's not like they accidentally pushed a button and six-million Jews were sent to the gas chambers. Sir, the Nazis are responsible for the deaths of about thirty million people throughout Europe, twenty-million from Russia alone. There is no forgiveness for that. The Germans own that. As for any living Nazis, they should be prosecuted along with those who benefited from the Nazis. Another thing, I'll never understand how any Jewish person can even bring him- or herself to own a German car. It's so unconscionable. As far as I'm concerned, the Germans should be forced to fund every humanitarian relief operation around the globe for a thousand years, the length of time Hitler wanted for his Thousand-Year Reich."

Mr. Rosenfeld seemed taken aback by my rant. There was a look of thunderstruck disbelief his face. I wasn't sure whether I overstepped my bounds, but I just had to say what I had to say. I understood where Nathalie was coming from. As far as I was concerned, she had fought the good fight and died for it. She dedicated her life to retrieving every valuable the Nazis had stolen from her grandfather. There was a passion about her, and she believed wholeheartedly in what she considered to be a righteous cause, and I would agree with that. I can't help but have the utmost respect and admiration for someone like that. She lived a life worth living, and there's nothing more honorable than dying for a cause in which one believes so wholeheartedly.

After several moments of absolute silence, Mr. Rosenfeld finally managed to speak. "David, it's eerie how much you sound like my daughter. Listening to you just then, those were exactly the types of comments she used to make. I can't understand how the two of you are so much alike. It's as if the both of you were cut from the same cloth or something."

"Mr. Rosenfeld, when I saw Nathalie in the restaurant yesterday, I felt some strange connection to her. It was as if we knew each other or something. I'm convinced that it was no coincidence that our paths crossed. I was meant to see your daughter yesterday. I was supposed to see the handoff, and then I was supposed to follow so that I could bear witness to her murder. I can't make sense of any of this, but it feels like I'm supposed to pick up where she left off. Every bone in my body is telling me that there's something waiting to be discovered."

"David, please, I implore you not to involve yourself. Whoever killed Nathalie will not hesitate to kill you as well."

"It's too late. I'm already involved," I replied.

Mr. Rosenfeld shot back, "It's not your battle."

"Mr. Rosenfeld, I can't thank you enough for taking the time to meet with me. I need to head out now, but I have a feeling we're going to be seeing each other again."

48

THOUGH DETECTIVE LORENZO had turned over to the FBI the case files, he had no intention of dropping the investigation. He held two critical pieces of evidence the feds didn't know about: the partial plate number of the van and Walker's glove.

The detective knew that if he queried the license plate number in the New York Department of Motor Vehicles database, the feds would be alerted, as they had when he entered Walker's information into the NYPD's database. The glove, on the other hand, should be able to be kept under the radar.

Dr. Carlisle was waiting for Detective Lorenzo when he arrived at the ME's office. The detective had called ahead to explain that he wanted the glove to be tested for cyanide residue. The residue on the glove, unlike that which enters the body, doesn't denature, and therefore it can still be detected.

It was after the detective departed the ME's office that it happened. He had just sat behind the wheel of his unmarked Taurus, feeling quite satisfied with himself for thinking he was one step ahead of the feds, when he heard a metal tapping on the passenger window.

The metal turned out to be the silencer attached to the barrel of a nine-millimeter Beretta handgun. The man holding the weapon, wearing a black fedora and with the coldest ice-blue eyes the detective had ever seen, motioned for him to unlock the passenger door. With the business end of the barrel pointing at his head through the window, the detective had no choice but to cooperate.

The killer was calm and cool. It was made clear to the detective that this would be the one and only warning. "Drop the investigation. It's in the hands of your FBI now." The English this man spoke was flawless but not native. The killer, in clear and certain terms, cautioned the detective that if he didn't, his two boys on Long Island would grow up without a father and his wife would become a widow. With the message delivered, the killer exited the vehicle, and the detective, knowing that he was outmatched, didn't even consider reaching for his own nine-millimeter Smith & Wesson.

49

SHORTLY AFTER DAVID departed the Rosenfeld's residence, the family friend from the Israeli Consulate stopped by the residence to express his condolences to the family. Earlier in the week, after Nathalie received the call from the Russian, she reached out to Yonatan to see if he could watch over her during the rendezvous. As much as she disregarded her father's concerns, deep down she knew the dangers.

Yonatan had steadfastly refused to involve himself or the Mossad in her scheme to blackmail the Russians. That was a bad idea in itself, but when coupled with the fact that Nathalie was in possession of those account numbers, he knew to keep as much distance between himself and Nathalie as possible. Like Nathalie's father, Yonatan also tried to talk her out of meeting the Russian, but of course she refused to heed his advice.

Claude knew that Yonatan had refused Nathalie's request to accompany her to the rendezvous, but he made it clear that he in no way held him responsible for Nathalie's death. Yonatan already knew this but appreciated Claude making a point of saying it. They both knew that Nathalie was off on a tangent, and it was only a matter of time before something happened to her. What the Israeli didn't tell Claude was that Nathalie had contacted him two weeks earlier about the list of names and account numbers from the Black Eagle Trust.

Claude shared with Yonatan the fact that the sole witness to Nathalie's murder, a young man by the name of David Walker, had been by the residence to pay his respects. Walker's name didn't click with Yonatan immediately, but after leaving the Rosenfeld residence, he found himself repeating the name to himself, as if trying to remember how he knew that name.

When Yonatan returned to the Israeli Consulate, as the CIA and SVR had done in the past twenty-four hours, Yonatan also entered David Walker into his agency's database to check for a match. Yonatan was floored when the Mossad file on Walker populated the screen. Yonatan couldn't even believe what he was reading. It was the same David Walker who had reported his neighbor to the SWC years earlier. Yonatan immediately recognized the name of the neighbor as being one of the names on the list of account numbers from the Black Eagle Trust that Nathalie had shared with him.

After Walker called the center, having identified a high-ranking SS official hiding in plain sight, a recording of the conversation made its way to the Israelis. Yonatan had been one of a handful of intelligence officers at the Mossad to be in the loop on this. Yonatan clearly remembered the conversation, not because this teenager had outed a senior SS officer but because of an astonishingly prescient offhanded remark the teenager made about his German neighbors. Walker had told the researcher that his neighbors "carried themselves as if the Nazis had won the war, not lost it." Walker could have never imagined that with that simple remark he had unknowingly solved the biggest conspiracy of the twentieth century.

For the life of him, the Israeli couldn't understand how fourteen years later, Walker had somehow come full circle on that remark, seemingly by sheer coincidence, and now was on the verge of learning the truth about Adolf Hitler's deception and his secret plot against America. As far as the Israeli was concerned, David had earned the right to know.

50

"DAVID, WHERE ARE you?" asked Detective Lorenzo.

"I'm with your guys. We're heading back to the Rosenfeld's residence," I replied.

"I thought you were there earlier?" asked the detective.

"I was, but he just called me again; apparently a family friend from the Israeli Consulate wants to talk to me," I replied.

"David, I'm off the case. Your friend, Mr. Blue Eyes, just paid me a visit."

"What happened?"

"When I was leaving the ME's office, he got into my car. He simply told me that this was my one and only warning. If I didn't drop the cases, he told me that my kids would grow up without a father," said the detective.

"At the precinct this morning, I gave you the contact information for the FBI special agent who is now in charge of the cases. You need to deal with him going forward. I'm off the case. David, I'm giving you some advice: you should just forget about what you saw. Mr. Rosenfeld was right. The case is never going to get solved. It's only been a day and already the FBI, CIA, the Russians, and now the Israelis are involved. It has danger written all over it."

"Detective, I appreciate your concern, but it's too late for me to run and hide. It's past that point. I'm just going over there to talk, nothing else."

"David, I can't stop you, but just don't do anything stupid." And then the detective hung up.

51

NOT LONG AFTER leaving the Rosenfeld's residence, Mr. Rosenfeld called me to ask if I could return for a meeting with a family friend who was interested in talking to me. It sounded intriguing.

When I returned to the residence, Mr. Rosenfeld escorted me back to the study where we spoke earlier. The family friend, named Yonatan, was already in the room, waiting for my arrival.

"David, I'd like you to meet Yonatan. He's been a friend of the family for years. He works at the Israeli Consulate here in Manhattan," said Mr. Rosenfeld.

"Hello, Yonatan, nice to meet you," I said as we shook hands.

"If you don't mind, I'm going to excuse myself and leave the two of you alone so you can have some privacy," said Mr. Rosenfeld as he saw himself to the door and closed it behind him.

It was doubtful that Yonatan was a true consular officer. My guess right off the bat was that he was Mossad. Everyone in the world of espionage and diplomacy knows that diplomatic missions worldwide are used as cover for spies. It actually makes sense given that their diplomatic status gives them immunity from prosecution for whatever they might be up to.

After Mr. Rosenfeld left the room, Yonatan's first words to me were, "So you're *the* David Walker. I've heard so much about you."

Why did he use a grammatical article before my name? I wondered.

"You don't even realize how deep you are in this, do you?" asked Yonatan.

"Look, my being at the restaurant was only a coincidence—wrong place, wrong time," I said, even though I felt that it was more like the right place at the right time, but I didn't care to get into that.

"I'm not talking about yesterday, David. The Israeli government has known about you for years. After yesterday though, you've managed to add a whole other layer of intrigue to your biography."

"What are you talking about?" I replied.

"We have known about you since August twenty-first, 1985," Yonatan replied. "That was the day you decided to call the Simon Wiesenthal Center (SWC) about your neighbor. Your war criminal of a neighbor lived in plain sight for thirty-five years without anyone ever suspecting anything. That is, until you decided to make that fateful call to the SWC. By the way, that's also the same day you came to the attention of your own CIA."

It felt like the bottom of my stomach fell out. I could barely breathe. "The center told me that my neighbor hadn't done anything of significance during the war," I replied.

"David, you were right about your neighbor. The researcher lied to you for your own safety. The truth is, your neighbor was very senior in the SS."

"What did he do during the war?" I asked.

"He was a lieutenant with SS Einsatzgruppen." The SS Einsatzgruppen were the mobile killing units that were deployed to Poland and the Soviet front.

"I knew he had blood on his hands; I just knew it," I replied. "Why are you telling me this now? What does that have to do with Nathalie?"

"Be patient. I'm getting to that," replied Yonatan. You unknowingly put yourself in danger by calling the center. Your call actually sent shockwaves through the CIA, among other intelligence services."

The Israeli's tone was very serious as he continued speaking. I knew that it was a time for listening, not talking.

"After the war, with the assistance of the CIA, your neighbor was resettled in the United States along with thousands of other hardcore SS like himself. However, your neighbor, along with a select group of others, weren't just any SS. They were special."

"This is where Nathalie comes in. Nathalie wasn't killed because she was trying to retrieve her family's artworks from the Russians. That was only a convenient pretext to get the Russians to do what the CIA needed done. Nathalie was killed because she acquired a secret list of World War II–era names and account numbers that were part of the Black Eagle Trust. This trust was established by a rogue element within the OSS and was used to transfer funds to Adolf Hitler's most loyal SS officers who had relocated to the United States and around the globe at the end of the war. Nathalie was killed because the list threatened to expose the OSS's sordid relationship between Adolf Hitler, America's shadow government, and the British royal family. The list would have also revealed Heinrich Himmler's handpicked SS conspirators behind Adolf Hitler's secret plot against America. That's why Nathalie had to be killed."

"Let me guess. This is where my neighbor comes in?"

"David, your neighbor is one of Hitler's conspirators. He's on the list obtained by Nathalie. When you were identified as the witness and the connection to your neighbor was realized, the odds of that happening were so astronomical that it had to be considered that you and Nathalie were working together."

"That's why the Russians were dispatched to kidnap and interrogate you. It needed to be established what exactly you knew.

"You might be wondering why the Russians, the same ones who had no compunction about killing Nathalie, were concerned enough about your health to rush you to the hospital. That's because there's someone at the CIA who is looking out for your well-being. This person had given the Russians strict instructions that you weren't to be killed."

"Yonatan, I don't want to sound unappreciative for you sharing this information with me, but I don't understand why you're telling me this."

"I'm sharing this information with you because it's the least I can do. After all, part of the reason you're in this situation is because you called the SWC to report your Nazi neighbor. Then yesterday, despite the dangers, you came forward to report to the police what you saw.

Lastly, before our meeting, I spoke with your protector at the CIA.
The both of us knew that if we didn't share the information with you,
given what we already know about you from your file, you would just
continue searching for answers to questions that you already know
the answers to."

"What are you talking about?"

The Israeli reminded David that when he called the Simon
Wiesenthal Center back in 1985, he made the astute observation:
"My neighbors carry themselves as if the Nazis won the war, not lost
it." It was then that the Israeli revealed Adolf Hitler's deception and
his secret plot against America.

52

IN THE FIELD of psychology, there is a theory called cognitive dissonance. Essentially what this means is that humans strive to maintain a certain internal harmony with regard to their established beliefs. If, however, new information is learned that contradicts what a person has held as a core truth, then this newly learned conflicting information causes psychological distress and disharmony (i.e., dissonance) within that person.

In order to reduce or eliminate this internal distress and thus regain or maintain a balanced harmony, the person will reject the new information learned, regardless of whether or not the new information is the truth. Time and time again, it has been shown that humans would prefer to continue believing a lie rather than accept the truth because of the disharmony it would cause.

53

There is no greater danger than
underestimating your enemy.

—Lao Tzu

AS COUNTERINTUITIVE AS it will seem, it was always Adolf
Hitler's strategy to lose World War II. It was never Hitler's intention to
militarily defeat the United States, but to defeat America from within.

To accomplish this, Hitler needed to create a scenario in which
thousands of his most loyal SS officers, serving as a Nazi Fifth column, would be allowed to infiltrate the US government and corporate
America after the war. The only way this could happen was if America,
and the world for that matter, was deceived into believing that the
Nazis had been soundly defeated and thus no longer posed a threat.

This puts Adolf Hitler's decision to invade the Soviet Union, aptly
named Operation Barbarossa, into an entirely different context. It's
important to note that Barbarossa was the name of the medieval

Holy Roman emperor Frederick Barbarossa of the year 1155, which German legend claims will restore Germany's greatness, which is significant given how important this operation was to Hitler's deception.

Adolf Hitler's suicidal decision to invade the Soviet Union was nothing more than a shrewd ruse to draw the Soviets into the war, thereby creating the situation at war's end in which a defeated Germany was occupied in the west by the United States, Great Britain, and France, and in the east by the Soviet Union. This perfectly laid the foundation for the Cold War confrontation between the United States and the Soviet Union. It was this context in which the Nazis were welcomed to the United States and around the world with open arms because in defeat, they were no longer viewed as a threat. This was exactly what Hitler wanted the Americans and the world to believe. "Deceive the heavens to cross the ocean," says another ancient Chinese military stratagem.

The Nazis quite predictably went from being America's enemy to being its most valuable ally in the Cold War against the Soviet Union. It was then the responsibility of the OSS/CIA, replete with recruits from the families of America's aristocracy, the same ones who helped militarize the Third Reich in the first place, to resettle their Nazi friends to America after the war. This takes 'conflict of interest' to a whole new level.

With the help of the OSS/CIA, the Nazi conspirators behind Hitler's Fifth Column settled into their new lives in America. Once in America these Nazis thoroughly infiltrated the military, CIA, FBI, and virtually every government agency of significance. Once inside, these Nazis impressed their hosts with their vast knowledge of America's Cold War adversary. "Charm and ingratiate your enemy. When you have gained his trust, move against him in secret," goes the ancient Chinese military stratagem.

The remaining Nazis, with their reputations for developing Hitler's awe-inspiring next-generation military weapons, seamlessly transitioned to jobs throughout America's defense industry. This put them in a position to feed into the military-industrial complex.

It was from within the CIA that America's shadow government, in partnership with the Nazis, worked doggedly at every turn to undermine the US government at home and abroad. They did everything possible to escalate the Cold War against the Soviets. With control of the corporate-owned media, just like under the Third Reich, it was easy to brainwash the entire population, which allowed them to hijack America's agenda while at the same time putting the United States on a path for absolute financial ruin.

Since the end of World War II, Hitler's Fifth Column has metastasized throughout America. With the groundwork laid, the Nazis are now conspiring to do exactly what Hitler did with the Reichstag Decrees, which is to turn the United States of America, the world bastion of democracy, into a totalitarian state. This transition will be triggered by a national emergency or series of national emergencies that will be designed to threaten the security of the population. As Hitler knew, under the right circumstances, any population can be easily manipulated into giving up their much-cherished privacy and freedoms in the name of restoring security. "If tyranny and oppression come to this land, it will be in guise of fighting a foreign enemy," US President James Madison said.

It will surprise most Americans to know that the Federal Emergency Management Agency (FEMA), in the event of a national emergency, already has in place "Continuity of Government" (COG) plans under Executive Orders 10995 through 11005, which grants the authority to the president of the United States to declare a national emergency without congressional approval. "National emergency" is loosely defined but is considered to include terrorist attacks, man-made disasters, earthquakes, pandemics, any incident that involves mass casualties, or an incident that damages our nation's infrastructure—environmental, political, economic, or financial crises.

Once the president declares the national emergency, the FEMA COG plan calls for the US Constitution to be suspended. When the Constitution is suspended, martial law will then be declared, which then permits FEMA to take over government functions at the local, state, and federal levels and allows for the suspension of all individual freedoms and rights that were guaranteed under the Constitution. The COG plan then calls for the mass arrest of any American citizens who are deemed national security threats, the definition of which is vague at best. This will allow for anyone with a dissenting opinion to be taken into custody and held at FEMA camps. It's estimated that two million people will be rounded up and held at these camps. It's not yet known whether s'mores will be served at the camps. Perhaps the most controversial aspect of the COG plan will be that the private ownership of all firearms will be prohibited.

Whatever the national emergency will be, it will set everything in motion. It'll be something so well coordinated and reasoned that most of the American public will think martial law makes sense, given whatever has transpired. Once activated, the FEMA COG plan allows for the deployment across America of the US military and even foreign military units under the United Nations. FEMA will be in charge and they will call all the shots, without input from the president or the US Congress. With military troops patrolling the streets of America, it will only be a matter of time before the civilians are viewed as the enemy. This coupled with the fact that America is strewn with firearms of all sorts, it will only be a matter of time before a confrontation occurs and the entire situation will likely descend into chaos.

The political situation in America will then affect the financial situation. This will be the point when America's staggering level of debt will have devastating consequences. America's central bank is the Federal Reserve. It will no doubt surprise most Americans that the Federal Reserve is not part of the US government. Its chairman and board of directors are appointed by the president, but it is owned and controlled by private banks, the largest and by far the most powerful of which is the worldwide Rothschild banking dynasty, believed to be one of the factions of the secret society of the Illuminati, with the Nazis being another faction and Britain's royal family being yet another faction.

Another fact that will no doubt surprise most Americans is that the Federal Reserve has structured America's debt much like a Ponzi scheme, in which the funds raised by selling US government securities are being used to pay the interest due, but not the principal, of previously sold securities. This is the classic definition of a pyramid scheme. "It is well that the people of the nation do not understand our banking and monetary system for if they did, I believe there would be a revolution before tomorrow morning," Henry Ford said.

At the time of its own choosing, the Rothschild banking dynasty will deliver the fatal blow to America by cutting off credit to the US Federal Reserve, leaving the US government without credit. Without funds, the Federal Reserve will collapse, sending America's economy into a freefall. Given the political and financial uncertainties, US dollars, which are in circulation all around the world and are also held as foreign currency reserves by the central banks of a great many nations, will flood the market in a Niagara Falls–scale deluge.

Something else most people don't realize is that the US dollar, like the paper currencies of every country in the world, is a "fiat" currency, which means the currency is not backed by gold, silver, or any commodity. The value of currency is determined by the economic relationship between supply and demand.

The result will be that the value of the US dollar, which had been the figurative gold standard for all currencies around the world ever since the Bretton Woods conference in July 1944, will crash to the depths of the Marianas Trench. Americans will experience hyperinflation on the same scale that Germany experienced it from 1921 to 1924, which was also at a time when the Rothschild banking dynasty withheld credit from Germany. Germany then took matters into its own hands and printed marks around the clock. Flooding the economy with marks led to the exchange rate of the mark skyrocketing from 75 marks to 5 trillion marks to the US dollar. In Germany during that time, it took a wheelbarrow full of marks to purchase a loaf of bread.

There will be a last-ditch effort to shore up the US dollar by tapping into America's gold reserves, which are purportedly the largest in the world at 261 million ounces of gold. However, no audit has been conducted on the nation's gold reserves in decades. So when the time comes to tap into the gold reserves, another deep dark secret will likely be revealed. America's gold reserves are long gone.

In the wake of the political and financial collapse of America, the Nazi movement, which had gone underground after World War II as was always Hitler's plan, will reemerge as the paradigm-crushing Fourth Reich. This Fourth Reich will be the "Thousand Year Reich," which is simply a euphemism for a New World Order (NWO) in the form of a one-world totalitarian government.

54

IT IS AN absolute existential necessity, regardless of the cost, sacrifice, or loss of life, to do absolutely everything humanly possible to ensure that we not only preserve this "miracle of life" on earth but that we propagate this "gift of life" throughout the entire universe. This is humanity's raison d'être.

It's an inconvenient truth that all past and present living species, including humans, are on a path toward eventual extinction. This happens due to the inability of the species to adapt to changes in the earth's temperature, climate, changes in environment (pollution), or because they are outright killed. At a skyrocketing rate, humanity is slowly succumbing to the diseases that are linked to our polluted environment: cancer, leukemia, fertility problems and birth defects, asthma, allergies, autism, neurobehavioral disorders, immune deficiencies, respiratory infections, brain and nerve damage (lead poisoning), cholera, liver damage, and ALS (Lou Gehrig's disease), among so many others. It's only a matter of time before the earth's ecosystems become so toxic that humanity can no longer survive.

Simply speaking, the world as it is today is not sustainable for the long term. There are 195 independent and sovereign countries in the world, each of which is in pursuit of its own national self-interests, more often than not to the detriment of the others and to the detriment of humanity. This flawed paradigm is responsible for so many of the crises facing the globe today: war, overpopulation, unequal distribution of resources, pandemics and diseases, pollution, an environment in decline, famine and drought, and the list goes on and on. Unless the status quo changes, these crises will increase and the environmental conditions will further deteriorate, and all the while the world's population continues to grow at an exponential rate. At some point in the not-too-distant future, if action isn't taken to get the world's population under control, the world will descend into chaos as the global population competes for the earth's finite resources.

The survival of humanity, and all life on earth for that matter, is entirely dependent on a new and revolutionary paradigm emerging in the form of a New World Order (NWO), in which all 195 countries come under a one-world totalitarian government. In this NWO there would be: one government, no borders, no national identities, one language, one bank, one digital currency, one military, population control, equal distribution of resources, environmental protection, and a uniform set of laws governing the entire globe on all matters. Under a NWO, for the first time in history, the world's population would go from thinking as individuals in pursuit of their own self-interests to a scenario in which they see themselves not as individuals but collectively as a species, in which decisions are made based on what is best for the survival of humanity in perpetuity.

However, the preservation of life on earth is no guarantee of humanity's survival. Sixty-six million years ago an asteroid, six miles in diameter, collided with earth in the Yucatan Peninsula. The force of the impact was so great, it left a crater 110 miles in diameter and 12 miles deep. The sheer magnitude of the impact caused such a disruption in the climate and is believed to have caused the extinction of the dinosaurs, along with an estimated 75 percent of the earth's plant and animal life. Humanity is that vulnerable to being wiped off the face of the earth forever.

It was never intended that humanity remain solely on earth forever. To do so would be tantamount to keeping all of humanity's eggs in one basket. Life, by its very nature, is about outward growth, literally and figuratively. In fact, it is an absolute existential necessity that we do everything humanly possible to not just preserve this miracle of life on earth, but that we propagate this gift of life throughout the entire universe. This is the only way to ensure the survival of our species, in whatever form it may evolve, in perpetuity. It has always been humanity's destiny to colonize the universe. The science that will be learned while pursuing this existential endeavor will require delving into the mysteries of quantum physics, which then opens new realms and dimensions and holds the secrets of time travel, parallel universes, and to the tenth dimension, when absolutely everything will be possible.

The Nazis were working on these mysteries of the universe through quantum physics as far back as the 1920s. The Nazis dominate if not own the field of quantum physics and most certainly have been working underground on the projects since World War II, which would account for the significant increase in UFO sightings in America after the arrival of the Nazis. Those Nazis are so clever, on par with the British in this regard, that they probably finagled a way for the Americans to pay the bills, which are likely buried in the black-ops budget.

We need to become the masters of our domain—the masters of our universe. We must unwrap all the mysteries of the universe. This very likely can only be achieved through human genetic engineering, self-learning artificial intelligence, and robots with artificial intelligence. These will be the next phases of human evolution. It's more feasible to send robots rooted with artificial intelligence to colonize the universe than it would be to send humans, with all their vulnerabilities, to explore the stars.

To colonize the universe is humanity's raison d'être. If we fail, no matter the reason, then we will have squandered this miracle of life. It doesn't matter what we accomplish on earth, or how sophisticated and cultured of a society we become, nor how caring we are to our neighbors, if we aren't able to spread this gift of life. If we don't colonize the universe, then we as a species have failed to ensure our existence in perpetuity. It's that simple. We are either masters of our domain or nothing. This is our singular objective that must be achieved no matter the cost.

However, despite everything that is at stake, no nation on earth would be willing to surrender their country's sovereignty for a greater good. Those in power, those who benefit by the status quo, and those who hold the reins of power in their respective countries, would do everything humanly possible to make sure something as revolutionary as a "one-world government" would never happen. It's too hard for people to see beyond their own self-interests and national self-interests to see how we all need to come together as a species. The competition for resources, though it has its benefits in the short run, will in the long run destroy this planet and humanity with it.

This entire discussion is so esoteric in nature that very few people even understand the issues. It's way too important an issue to be left to any government, or even worse, to the will of the people.

55

IT WAS ALWAYS America's destiny to take the world closer to the New World Order. It's a well-known fact that President George Washington, along with most of the other Founding Fathers, were Freemasons. The Freemasons are a faction under the Illuminati. The Illuminati refers to the bloodlines of genetically related individuals from thirteen of the most powerful families, some of which reach back to the ancient world. By far the most powerful of these families is the Rothschild family, with an estimated worth of $500 trillion. The Rothschild banking dynasty has controlling ownership interests at all the central banks in the world (i.e., America's New York Federal Reserve) except for Cuba, North Korea, and Iran.

The official Seal of the United States of America, which was adopted in 1782, contains the Latin phrase *Novus Ordo Seclorum*— "New World Order." The seal also contains the Latin phrase *E. Pluribus Unum*, which means "out of many, one." It is often mistakenly believed that this refers to America as a "melting pot," but it actually refers to the nations of the world coming together under a NWO. Lastly, the phrase *Annuity Coeptis*, which means "Commencement" or "Undertaking," meaning this was America's purpose, to take the world to this NWO.

The Illuminati is known for its use of symbols, several of which can be found on the US one-dollar bill: all-seeing eye (Eye of Lucifer), pyramid (represents the top-down command structure of the Illuminati rulers of the universe), and owl (hidden on front is the symbol of Minerva, the goddess of wisdom). Illuminati and Freemason symbols can be found throughout Washington, DC, as well.

The goals of the Illuminati are for the abolition of all government, nationalism, private property, inheritance, family unit, and organized religion. Its most significant and controversial goal is its intention to reduce the world's population from the current seven billion down to a manageable five hundred million.

The Illuminati is by no means the only secret society, there are others: Knights Templar, Jesuits, Trilateral Commission, Bilderberg Group, among countless others. The stated goal of these secret societies, collectively known as the Worldwide Shadow Government, is for the establishment of a NWO in the form of a one-world totalitarian government. These are the societies that have been charting the course of civilization and world events ever since ancient times. They have their people strategically planted throughout governments, intelligence agencies, military, law enforcement, World Bank, World Trade Organization, International Monetary Fund, United Nations, banking, corporations, think tanks, and the list goes on and on.

They are everywhere and they are nowhere because these secret societies will never confirm their existence. That's what makes them secret. The individuals in these societies are those who are driven by a higher ideal. These are the people who are doing everything possible to ensure that this gift of life on earth is not squandered, but that we are able to propagate this gift throughout the universe. This is the role they play.

With this level of control, this Worldwide Shadow Government has been meticulously masterminding events throughout history in such a deliberate and calculated manner as to bring about this New World Order (NWO). The motto of the Illuminati is "Order out of Chaos." To accomplish this requires thousands of well-coordinated paradigm-changing events, throughout history, to take the world closer, one step at a time, to an NWO. It's chess on a global scale.

It will come as a surprise to many that it was American industrialists and bankers, along with the British and the Germans, who funded Vladimir Lenin's Bolshevik Revolution, which overthrew the Romanov Dynasty in Russia. Then once the Communists got into office, these Americans, British, and Germans identified Soviet Communism as the ultimate threat. The Cold War was planned well before it ever happened.

Another faction of the Illuminati is the British royal family. It's important to note that the British royals have German bloodlines. Their family name was originally Von Battenberg. However, after World War I, because of anti-German sentiment, they changed their name to the House of Windsor, which successfully hides their German roots. During the 1930s, the royal family were big supporters of Adolf Hitler, as were America's elite.

Yet another faction of the Illuminati from the American side was the Skull and Bones Society at Yale University. This secret society was brought over from Germany in 1832 and is believed to be a branch or faction of the Illuminati. Several American presidents were members of the Skull and Bones society. The Illuminati, in coordination with America's elite via the Skull and Bones Society, formed the Office of Strategic Services (OSS) and then the Central Intelligence Agency (CIA). The CIA is the Illuminati.

56

FOR THE LIFE in me I couldn't understand why the Israeli confirmed what I had suspected for some time. *He must have a motive*,
I thought. The Mossad is the best. Yonatan must have had an angle;
intelligence officers always do. Jamie is fond of using the proverb,
"Don't look a gift horse in the mouth." I can't stand that expression.

Horse traders are notoriously an unscrupulous lot to start with.
It would behoove the recipient of a "gift horse" not to inspect the
horse's mouth and take a look at the length of the teeth and gums.
The length of the teeth can be used to estimate the age of the horse,
and the condition of the gums will indicate whether the horse is
healthy. This small preventative measure of looking a gift horse in
the mouth can avert costly medical bills down the road for the new
owner. This small measure also serves to prevent the possibility of
a pretend giver from pawning off a sick horse on some naive and
unsuspecting person. This would be an insincere and costly gift at a
minimum, with all the benefit going to the giver. What I'm trying to
say is that I don't want to get played; it's that simple. So whenever
some says, "Don't look a gift horse in the mouth," I immediately think,
"White elephant."

"Yonatan, why on earth did you share this with me?" I asked, in the most incredulous tone.

"You sound unappreciative," replied Yonatan. "I thought you would be happy to know that you were right about your neighbor and about Hitler's conspiracy."

"They killed Nathalie for knowing what I know, so why on earth did you tell me?" I asked.

"David, it was your protector at the CIA who gave me permission to share part of it with you. He knew if we didn't tell you that you would only continue searching for answers. This would mean that it would only be a matter of time before you met the same fate as Nathalie. For whatever reason, he doesn't want anything to happen to you."

"Yonatan, that doesn't quite make sense."

"There is something else. You already knew too much before I even shared anything with you. They don't want you dead, but they need you under control. They need you to get under the umbrella of the CIA. This is their way of getting you under control. Otherwise, you'll always be considered a loose end. My sharing everything with you was done with the intention of forcing you in that direction. Now you definitely know too much not to join the agency. I'm sorry, but it had to be done. It's for your own good."

"I knew you were playing me."

"It wasn't like that. It was more like we're just forcing your hand."

"You must be joking. There's no chance I'm going to join the agency. They killed Nathalie."

"David, she was poking around those account numbers. That was like touching the third rail and not expecting to be hurt. Don't be stubborn. Your protector at the CIA said that you had applied there just a few years ago. You didn't get hired because they didn't have funding, but they were interested in you. They think you're a natural researcher and analyst. You have good intuition; you're able to connect dots where others see nothing. That's your gift! If you don't want to join the agency directly, they can find something for you elsewhere. Just join the agency. They are everywhere. They can find something for you."

"Yonatan, I can't commit to anything right now. I need to head out. There's something I need to take care of."

"What do you have to take care of?" the Israeli asked incredulously.

"I have an idea how I can finish what Nathalie started yesterday."

"What are you talking about?" asked Yonatan, with a puzzled look.

"It's a long shot, but I need to take care of something. What I'm doing has nothing to do with the CIA, but it will likely piss off the Russians," I said.

"What are you talking about? Don't be ridiculous! You're going to end up dead."

"I don't think so. If you can get to the Russians, just cover for me. Okay?"

"I'm telling you, don't do whatever it is you're thinking about doing."

"Yonatan, I gotta do what I gotta do. It's that simple. So please, just cover for me. After I'm done, I promise to drop everything, but I gotta take care of something."

And with that I departed the Rosenfeld residence.

Part 3

57

MY ATTENTION RETURNED to Nathalie. I was determined to finish what she had started yesterday. I had a crazy idea; it was a one-in-a-million hunch, but I had nothing to lose. When I spoke to Mr. Rosenfeld earlier, he mentioned that the Russian was only handing over to Nathalie a small sampling of the pictures to serve as proof that he did indeed possess evidence that the Russians were in possession of the family's artworks. If what was in that bulging envelope was only a small sampling, that meant there must have been a large stack of pictures in total. It occurred to me that it was unlikely that he traveled from Russia with all those pictures in his luggage. The risk of the pictures being discovered while passing through airport security checkpoints would have been too great. Another thing: given the nature of the pictures, it's doubtful he would have had the film developed while in Russia for fear of tipping off the film developer or anyone else to his plans.

It's quite plausible that he came to the United States with the rolls of film and then had them developed when he arrived in New York City. I had a friend who owned a photo studio that developed pictures, and I recalled how he mentioned that the photo-developers sometimes save pictures or negatives at the studio of nude shots or anything else that was out of the ordinary or just interesting. On occasion, they would even report certain pictures to police if they thought a crime had been committed. In the case of the Russian, whoever developed the pictures maybe thought it was suspicious that all these pictures were being taken of a trove of artworks from some storage unit, and given that the rolls of film were most likely a Russian brand, maybe just maybe it would have sounded enough of an alarm enough to warrant making extra copies of the prints or negatives. It was a long shot, but that was my hunch.

On a number of occasions in my adult life, when wearing an over-coat with a suit and tie, as I was that day, people have told me that I looked like an FBI special agent. Well, on this day I was going to test it. With that I jumped into a taxi and headed to Chinatown to find a place selling a half-decent fake FBI badge that I could use to pull off my plan. With badge in hand, I went to the Marriott Hotel in Times Square, where Nathalie's father had told me that the Russian had been staying, and started checking photo developing businesses in the area. It took four places before I found the business where the Russian had had the pictures developed, and as I suspected, copies of the negatives were saved. It's all about attitude. Because of the badge in my hand, the film developer was extremely cooperative and made a set of pictures, totaling 160 prints, and then handed over the negatives to me.

Shortly thereafter, for the third time that day, I found myself in Mr. Rosenfeld's study. Despite everything that had happened over the last twenty-four hours, I sat in the leather chair with what must have looked like a self-satisfied look of pride on my face while holding a plastic bag.

"What's in the bag, David?"

"I have all the pictures the Russian wanted to sell to Nathalie." I removed seven envelopes of pictures from the bag and then handed them to Nathalie's father.

When I handed Nathalie's father the picture envelopes, he had the most astonished look upon his face. Without saying a word, Mr. Rosenfeld started going through the pictures. After looking at only a handful of pictures, his eyes began to well up, and a tear rolled down his face.

"I remember these from my father's gallery," he said. "It's been so long ago, but it seems like yesterday. It's all coming back to me." He removed one of the pictures from the stack and showed me. "That painting hung in the family room of our home in Paris before the war. I was only five years old, but I remember that painting so well," he said. "David, how did you get these pictures?"

"It's a long story," I replied.

"David, please forgive me, but I don't understand. You were already in danger, so why would you then go out of your way to put yourself in deeper? It doesn't make any sense."

"Mr. Rosenfeld, now that you have the pictures, maybe your Israeli friend Yonatan could find a way to pressure the Russians into returning your family's paintings."

"I understand that, but why do you care about my family's artworks?"

"I did this for Nathalie, sir. I could think of no better way to avenge her death than to recover these pictures. I wanted to finish what she started. Maybe now Nathalie's soul might be at peace, knowing the artworks may at long last be returned to your family."

"David, but why? I'm absolutely mystified why you would go to such lengths for a woman you never even met."

"I never met Nathalie, but I'm certain that I know her, somehow. I'm certain of it."

58

Synchronicity is an ever-present reality
for those who have the eyes to see.

—Carl Jung

THERE ARE POWERS in the spiritual realm that are beyond humankind's comprehension. In this spiritual realm, all of humankind is interconnected, and there are no coincidences; everything that happens in our lives connects to the past, present, or future. It's only when we connect with our spiritual self, in mind, body, and spirit that we are able to recognize coincidences for the omens, good or bad, that they are. These omens are not something that we seek out ourselves, but rather it's the universe reaching out to us to communicate a message. These omens come in many forms, but if people are not connected with their spiritual selves, if they are not in sync with their souls, these messages being delivered to us by the universe will never be recognized nor understood for the omens of enlightenment that they are. It's only when people become one with themselves that they will ever understand their purpose in life.

Maktub is an Arabic word whose literal translation is "it is written." There is no equivalent in the English language, but the closest word is "destiny." But *maktub* refers to the belief that we all have an individual journey or path in life that is already known—"it is written"—and you must be true to yourself and follow this path, wherever it may lead. To follow your path is your singular purpose in life, never to be cast aside for anything. And when you commit to your journey, that's when you truly connect with your spiritual self. When you then commit to and believe with every sense of self, that's when the magic in life happens. "And, when you want something, all the universe conspires in helping you to achieve it," said Paul Coelho in *The Alchemist*.

David's seemingly chance encounter with Nathalie was no coincidence but a matter of sure and certain destiny. David and Nathalie had been on separate but parallel tracks their whole lives to uncover Hitler's deception. This was their destiny, and the laws of synchronicity brought them together. Fate had placed David in the restaurant that day so he could bear witness to Nathalie's killing and continue where she would leave off. And although they never met, David and Nathalie were kindred spirits, and the universe saw to it that their lives would intersect and that her death wouldn't be in vain.

59

BY THE TIME I returned to my apartment, it was seven o'clock that evening. Despite the torturous day, I was still going strong on pure adrenaline. I was awake in every sense of the word.

I still couldn't understand for the life of me how my chance encounter with Nathalie connected me back to my childhood neighbor, which then put me in the middle of Adolf Hitler's deception, something that I had long suspected. It made no sense. It was impossible to comprehend the number of coincidences that had to take place for that to have happened. Yonatan was right; it would be a waste of time to tell anyone because nobody would ever believe me.

With that thought on my mind, there was a faint knock on my door. "David, it's me, Susan. Are you home?" Rather than respond, I just opened the door and stepped aside so she could enter.

There had been so much going on during the day that I barely had time to think about the kiss we shared together this morning. Now that I was home, I knew we were going to pick up where we left off. Given the intensity of the past thirty-six hours, that was precisely what I needed.

"I thought I heard your door," said Susan. "How was your day? Did you learn anything?"

"I learned quite a bit actually, but not in a million years would you believe any of it."

"I'd believe anything you told me," replied Susan.

"We can save that conversation for another time," I responded.

"If you're hungry, I can order us a pizza or something."

"I'm fine for now," I replied.

"I'm home by myself tonight," said Susan, with a faint smile.

"Where is Kaitlyn?"

"She's staying at a friend's tonight."

"How did you manage that? Did you bribe her?"

"I think she wanted us to be alone tonight. I think she has been scheming this scenario for some time."

Without saying anything else, we leaned toward each other, and we kissed. The kiss quickly escalated from passionate to not being able to get enough of each other. Our hands were all over each other, and without our lips parting, in unison we lowered ourselves onto my bed. With me on top, I rolled slightly to her right side, thus making her entire body available. I held both her hands loosely above her head with my left hand, leaving my right hand free to wander.

She had the body of a ballerina. While kissing, my hand caressed her shoulder and down her arm, allowing our fingers to briefly interlace. My hand then glided across her sweater then circled back down across her stomach, reaching underneath her sweater and then under her bra. I massaged her small and firm breasts and gently pinched her nipples; they came to life. Releasing her hands with my left hand, my hand disappeared underneath her shoulder blades and as she arched her back, my fingers unsnapped the bra clasp with a quick flick. She briefly sat up and raised her hands above her head, and I removed her sweater and bra in one motion. She lay back, and I kissed her breasts, my tongue surveying her perfectly formed pink areolas, and ever-so-gently nibbled her hardened nipples with just the right amount of pressure.

Susan's whole body was writhing in anticipation. While kissing her breasts, my right hand wandered farther down across her stomach across her flattened pelvis. Her knees were bent and angled in opposite directions. Her skirt was gathered around her waist, exposing her simple white cotton panties. My hand careened across her pelvis and then veered off along the inside of her thighs, then to her knee, then calf, to her foot, and then all the way back up once again along her inner thigh and veering off at the last moment, wanting her anticipation to build to the point that she couldn't take it any longer. It was at that moment that she reached down to remove her panties, which I had made such an effort to stay clear of, but I placed my hands over hers and whispered, "I want to be the one to take off your panties."

"Please, don't make me wait anymore!" said Susan as she lifted her hips slightly off the bed and gyrated her pelvis upward. I placed the palm of my hand over her panties and rubbed slowly yet with pressure from the outside. I lowered myself between her legs and kissed her inner thighs, alternating from one to the other, as close to her panties as possible without touching. I then kissed her through her panties. Her whole body came alive, writhing and squirming, and her legs splayed apart. I led her right hand down across her stomach to her panties and guided her fingers under the elastic band and had her pull her panties to the side for me. It was entirely shaved and was as beautiful. With my right hand, I reached underneath her thigh for her left hand and interlaced our fingers and then gently placed a kiss at the top of her flower, first with closed mouth, which turned into a slow French kiss. I did everything possible to make Susan feel like she was at the center of the universe.

Kneeling on the bed, I pulled her legs toward me. She instinctively raised her hips, and I reached down with both hands and with measured movement removed her panties. I don't know what happened to her skirt, but it wasn't around her waist any longer. "I want you inside me," she said, and with that she swung her body around and undid my pants. With one tug my pants went down, exposing my fully erect member. She immediately devoured it, all lips and tongue, no teeth, and with the right amount of saliva. It felt amazing.

"I want you inside me, David," she said as she lay on her back with her legs apart, motioning for me to enter. In a slow and deliberate motion, I could feel each and every inch slowly disappear inside of her, and then we were one.

60

AS WE LAY in bed, with Susan's head resting on my chest, I noticed that my cell phone on the bedside table was blinking from a missed call. I had silenced the phone when Susan came over. I reached for the phone and saw that there were eight missed calls, two from Jamie and six from her father. Why was the governor calling, I wondered. *There's no way he could know about the past thirty-six hours*, I thought. Or could he?

"Susan, I hate to do this, but I need to call Jamie. She and her father have been trying to reach me. Don't leave though; the call will only take a minute. I'm so sorry."

"Don't worry about it. It's okay. I can go back to my place while you make the call, if you want," replied Susan.

"No, that isn't necessary. I'll be quick." And with that I placed a quick kiss on her lips. "I hope everything was as amazing for you as it was for me."

"I loved everything, absolutely everything. I needed that. I feel like a new woman. We can talk more about it later. I know you need to call whatchamacallit." Susan never called Jamie by name, and Jamie would never say Susan's name, only referring to her as Kaitlyn's mother. It was just an observation.

"Okay, I'll be quick." I dialed Jamie's number.

"Hello, Jamie, what's going on?"

"David, what have you been doing? My father has been trying to reach you. It's something really serious. Why haven't you been answering your telephone? David, he's really upset. You gotta call him immediately."

I knew with certainty that the governor knew. I had no idea how he could have known, but that's the governor. He knows things you could never imagine he knew. That's probably why I consider him the smartest person I've ever known.

"Jamie, somehow my phone went into silence mode. I never knew anyone was trying to reach me."

She was clearly annoyed and skeptical of my "silence mode" excuse, but she didn't push the issue. That would no doubt come later.

"David, just call my father and call me back when you're done. I wanna know what's going on."

"Okay, I'll call him and then call you back."

"David, what's going on?" asked Susan.

"I'm not sure. I need to call Jamie's father. He's been trying to reach me, and it probably has something to do with something I did today."

"What did you do?" asked Susan.

"It's hard to explain, but I need to call her father. Don't leave though; it'll only take a few minutes."

"It's okay. I understand."

"Thanks. It'll only be a minute." With that I dialed.

"Hello, Governor, it's me, David." He didn't give me a chance to say another word.

"What the fuck are you doing down there?" That was the first time I ever heard the governor say the word "fuck." He yelled a lot but seldom swore.

I was reluctant to say anything until I knew what he knew. "What? What are you talking about?"

"Don't give me that! I just got a call from a very important person about you. You've gotten yourself into a very serious situation—very serious."

"Governor, I swear to you, it's not what it seems!"

"Not what it seems? David, it's way past that. You're in danger. You're in real danger. I was told you handed over some highly sensitive Russian documents to someone. What are you doing?"

"Governor, they weren't documents. They were pictures of artworks that had been stolen by the Nazis but ended up with the Russians."

"David, that doesn't matter. Right now the Russians are livid about what you did."

"Should I be worried?"

"David, it's past that." His voice trailed off. "You're in serious trouble. The only reason you're not in even more serious trouble is because someone I haven't seen in decades stuck his neck out for you because of your connection to me. That's the only reason. He wants to meet with you tomorrow."

"Governor, the past thirty-six hours have been by far the most fucked up hours of my entire life. Are you sure I'll be safe?"

The governor fell silent after I posed that question. If it were someone else, I would have thought that the line dropped, but because I was speaking to him, I knew the silence was one of his trademark pregnant pauses. I learned long ago never to talk while he was trying to formulate a thought. *Just let him work it through*, I thought. The Governor had such a talent for finding solutions to problems. I had total confidence that he would come up with something.

"David, I'm coming down tomorrow. We'll attend the meeting together. Are you okay with that?"

"Yes, that works! Thank you."

"I'll be at your apartment by seven a.m. The meeting isn't until nine o'clock, but I don't want to take a chance with getting stuck in traffic. Besides, that'll leave us time for you to explain how the hell you got yourself into this mess in the first place."

"Okay, Governor, that's a good plan. Thank you again."

"Okay, let me go now. I need to call the colonel to see if I can get a trooper for the morning." The colonel the governor was referring to was the superintendent of the Rhode Island State Police (RISP). One of the perks of being a former governor was that the Rhode Island State Police, on special occasions, made a state trooper and vehicle available to him.

"I'll see you in the morning, David."

"Good night, Governor." And with that the call ended.

Before I could return to bed, Susan spoke. "David, is everything okay? Are you in trouble or something?" asked Susan, with concern in her voice.

"I'm sure you gathered from the call that the governor is coming in the morning. We're going to attend a meeting together. It'll be okay, but I might have overstepped a few boundaries today. Everything will be fine."

"What did you do?"

"It's a long story. We can talk about it another time. For now, why don't we take a shower and then get back to what we were doing earlier?"

"Good idea."

61

I AWOKE FIRST that morning but lay still as to not awaken Susan. It was slowly coming back to me. I had had a dream; it was so surreal. *Could it be?* I thought. I was trying to make sense of something that made no sense, not in a linear universe anyway. It was then that Susan awoke. Analyzing the dream would have to wait. It had already been about 180 years in the making, so it could wait just a little bit longer.

"Good morning, beautiful!"

Without opening her eyes, but with a smile on her face, Susan rolled on top of me. We wrapped our arms around each other, and with my hand, I moved her reddish hair away from her face.

"Last night was so incredible," said Susan, in a satisfying tone.

"It was very long overdue," I added. "I think that contributed to the passion. I hope you enjoyed last night as much as I did."

"I certainly did. That was a neat trick you taught me. Had I known how painless it was and how amazing it felt, I would have been doing that long ago. You took missionary to a whole new level," said Susan.

"We could have done anything whatsoever last night, and it would have been beautiful," I told her. "That's how right everything felt."

"I agree. We certainly did more than I've ever done in the bedroom, that's for sure. I wish we could stay in bed all day and do it all again."

"So do I, but unfortunately, I need to get ready," I said as I leaned in to give her a kiss.

"David, I just want to tell you that I understand that this might be the only time we're together. I'm just happy that we'll always have this shared experience."

"Thank you for being so understanding. I'm not sure what's next for me, but I'm happy we were able to share ourselves with each other like that," I replied.

"How will you handle this with Kaitlyn? Will she understand."

"David, she's an old soul. She understands everything. She knows it's only a matter of time before you head overseas to work. In a perfect world, she would want us together, but she knows the situation. She'll be fine."

"Okay. That makes it easier. I need to shower and get dressed."

"While you're getting ready, I'll make us breakfast. Sound good?"

"Sounds terrific," I replied.

62

THE RHODE ISLAND State Police (RISP) cruiser pulled up to the curb outside my apartment on Sixty-Third Street as I was watching out the window. Despite the gravity of the situation, it brought a smile to my face seeing the governor in the passenger seat of the cruiser. The governor always knew how to make an entrance.

"Governor, this is David. I saw you pull up. I'll be right down."

As I exited my apartment building, I walked up the sidewalk for about ten feet and then turned back toward the cruiser so that I could approach in full view of the governor and trooper. I wanted them to see me coming rather than just appearing out of a blind spot. Just two days earlier it would have never occurred to me to do that. When the governor saw me, he wasn't smiling. He just motioned with a flick of his hand to get in the back seat.

"Good morning, Governor, Trooper!"

Talk about irony. The RISP winter uniforms look like they came right out of Nazi-era Germany: high chestnut brown boots, dark charcoal-gray wool breeches, long-sleeve charcoal-gray shirt with a black tie and a military-campaign style felt hat, tan. The uniform wouldn't be complete without the three-quarter-length heavy leather coat, which was also brown and matched the boots. The troopers are usually physically formidable to start with—six feet used to be the minimum height requirement. In these uniforms the troopers cast a very imposing presence. The RISP was founded in 1925, and had always been considered more of a paramilitary organization than a police department. Anyhow, they're considered Rhode Island's premier apolitical law enforcement agency and are highly respected.

The governor was clearly annoyed and didn't bother to reply, but the trooper cast a quick look at me to say, "Hello, David."

"Trooper, I'm going to sit in the back seat with David, so I don't end up with a sore neck."

"That's fine, Governor."

The governor got out of the car and opened my door and shooed me with his hand to move over.

"Trooper, we're heading to the Scobee Diner in Little Neck. You know how to get there?"

"Yes, Governor, I know the city. That's why the colonel chose me. He didn't want a repeat of your trips to Boston."

The Israeli had told me that it was someone at the CIA who was looking out for my well-being, so I assumed this was the same person who called the Governor about me. Obviously we weren't going to meet at CIA offices at the World Trade Center.

"David, I need to hear it from you. What is this all about?"

I shared the entire story with the governor, except for what the Israeli told me about Hitler's deception. I still hadn't processed that part myself. Regardless, that wasn't something I ever intended to discuss with the governor anyway. It wasn't my place to ever raise that topic with him. I didn't even want to know whether or not he knew. Sometimes there are secrets that should never ever be repeated, and this was one of them.

"What have you told Jamie?" asked the Governor.

"I barely mentioned anything to her. She knows I saw Nathalie collapse on the sidewalk and that I spoke to a detective about it. But she knows nothing about the kidnapping or anything else. The situation got so complicated so fast, it would have taken too much explaining. Sometimes it's easier to say nothing."

"You're right about that. Well, I'm glad she doesn't know anything, being a reporter and all. That makes the situation easier to manage."

When we pulled into the parking lot of the Scobee Diner, the governor could tell I was a little nervous. He reassured me that everything was going to be fine. If I hadn't trusted the governor as much as I did, I might have suspected something was amiss, given the fact that we weren't meeting at the CIA's offices.

"Governor, is the trooper coming in with us?"

"No, that isn't necessary. He will wait with the car. David, everything will be fine. This person only wants to have a few words with you."

63

SCOBEE DINER WAS a mainstay for the community in Queens ever since the 1960s. It was opened by Greek immigrants but without the distinct cultural elements of their roots. It was the place that little league teams went to celebrate championships, where reunions were held, and where many in the area went for first dates. The diner had a blue-collar feel but was enjoyed by all.

When we entered the diner, tables occupied by patrons were sprawled across the open floor, with booths along the wall to the right and the counter to the left. It looked to be a full house.

The governor saw him first. The man was in the corner booth. He stood and waved to get the governor's attention.

"Stay here. I want to have a few words with him first," said the governor.

"Sure, of course." *Anything to stall the inevitable.*

I watched as the governor approached the man, who looked to be maybe twenty years the governor's junior. They greeted each other like old acquaintances, with a firm handshake and warm smiles. *If there was going to be trouble, the man wouldn't have been smiling*, I thought. That was a good sign.

They didn't sit but remained standing at the booth as they spoke. It looked as though they were catching up a bit; then after about five-minutes, I could tell the conversation had shifted by the seriousness that came across their faces. They spoke for another few minutes before the governor waved me over.

"David, I'd like you to meet Dick Worthington. Dick, this is David Walker."

"It's nice to meet you, Mr. Worthington." I made a point not to allude to the fact that the Israeli referred to him as being the person who made sure no harm came to me.

"I'm glad you could come, David."

"It seemed like the right thing to do," I replied, with a slight smile.

"You're in good hands, David. I'm going to give you two some pri-vacy. I'll be at the counter," said the governor.

"We won't be long," Dick said to the governor.

"David, please sit," said Dick as he gestured with his hand for me to sit in the booth. He sat facing the entrance, and I sat with my back toward the door. "I want you to know that the only reason we're even meeting is because of the governor."

"I appreciate that. Thank you."

"I'm not here to talk about anything from the last few days. I'm only here because I want to offer you a job. You're a natural researcher and analyst. What you have learned and the dots you've been able to connect—you've figured out things that nobody else has figured out. You would be an asset at the agency, and we'd be lucky to have you onboard. You know yourself that you're wasting your time at Lucent."

"I'm there because nothing else worked out. I applied to the agency a few years back but didn't get hired. That's why I was forced to enter the private sector."

"For the record, we wanted to hire you, but we just didn't have the funding. By the time funding was restored, you had already pulled your application."

"Mr. Worthington, I need some time to think about it. After the last few days and what happened to Nathalie, I'm not sure what I want to do."

"David, those feelings are understandable. You've been through a lot in the past two days, but let me be clear. You know too much to not join the agency. You'd be 'a loose end,' and there are other organizations out there who would not tolerate you not being under the agency umbrella, in whatever capacity. They need to know that we have you under control. But if you go off and do your own thing, then I'm afraid it won't end well for you."

"Mr. Worthington, I'm not sure it would be a good fit any longer. Everything is about compartmentalization there. I'd never know what was going on. That would be torture. I'm always trying to figure out the big picture. That's just what I do. It wouldn't be good. I'd be trying to solve every conspiracy in the world. I want to know where we're heading. Not just today, but in fifty years, one hundred years, and a thousand years out. What's the endgame? If I joined I would constantly be trying to learn the real truth, and I know how far down the truth is buried. I'd be digging and digging. It would be counter-productive, and at the same time, I refuse to be a mindless cog in the wheel."

"What is it with you always researching and searching for answers that nobody else even cares about? Where does that come from?"

"Have you ever seen the movie *Raiders of the Lost Ark*, with Harrison Ford? The movie came out in the early 1980s, maybe in 1981. I was about thirteen years old at the time."

"Yes, I know the movie. What about it?" replied Mr. Worthington as he leaned back in the booth to listen.

In the movie, Harrison Ford plays a renowned archeologist named Indiana Jones who is in search of the Ark of the Covenant, which is thought to be the resting place of the Ten Commandments, the actual stone tablets. Anyhow, the story is set in the late 1930s, and Adolf Hitler is in search of ancient relics of the occult from all around the world. The Nazis are searching for the Ark of the Covenant, but Harrison Ford finds the Ark first in the ancient city of Tanis, but the Nazis steal it from him. Long story short, Harrison Ford steals it back and then turns it over to the US government so it can be studied. However, the government does not plan on studying this incredible historical find, only putting the Ark into storage.

"Do you recall the second-to-last scene of the movie? It shows the wooden crate containing the Ark of the Covenant being placed into storage in a massive warehouse the size of several football fields, packed with millions of other crates," I asked.

"Yeah, I remember." Mr. Worthington clearly had no idea where I was going with this.

"I can remember when I saw all those crates in the warehouse, I tried to imagine what could possibly be in all those crates. I remember thinking to myself, I want to be the one who knows all the secrets."

"Mr. Worthington, that's who I am. That's who I've always been. Regardless of whether or not I join the agency, I think it's incumbent upon the agency to make sure nothing happens to me."

"What are you talking about, David?"

"I'm talking about the quote that the CIA has etched on its wall at headquarters: 'And ye shall know the truth and the truth shall make you free.' That's precisely what I've done. I haven't stolen government secrets to figure out what I figured out. I used all open sources. Call me naive, but in my opinion, the agency needs to honor that."

"David, it's more complicated than that. Here, take my card," he said as he handed me his business card. "Take some time to think about what we discussed, and then call me, either way."

"Mr. Worthington, I sincerely thank you for looking out for me these last few days. The governor and Yonatan both made it clear that I owe you a debt of gratitude."

"You're welcome, David. I look forward to hearing from you."

64

THE GOVERNOR AND I returned to the cruiser. "David, do you need to be in for work today?"

"Governor, after the past few days, I'm never returning there. I'm done with that job."

"Let's take a ride to Hartford to see Jamie. We can go for lunch or something."

The governor made the call to Jamie from the car. She was going to free herself up around noon to join us for lunch. I wasn't entirely looking forward to seeing Jamie because I knew she was going to drill me for answers to further explain why I missed her calls last night. At least her father would be present, so she would only be able to take that line of questioning so far.

"David, it's a shame you can't share what you've been through the last two days. That would have made an incredible story for the book you've said you always wanted to write."

"Do you think it would be an issue if I didn't use any names and listed it as fiction? Nobody would ever suspect that it was the truth," I explained, "but then I would at least be able to say I told you so when everything unfolds."

"David, I hope you're not serious. You can't write about any of this, but if you ever do, please don't write it while I'm alive."

"I was just thinking aloud. I doubt I would ever write about it," I explained.

"What's going on with Jamaica? I spoke to the travel agency yesterday, and they told me you hadn't booked your flight yet."

"To be honest, I'm not sure about going. Jamie and I are having relationship difficulties, so I'm not sure if now is a good time."

"Then go for counseling."

"If we're not even married and we're already going to counseling, then I think that's a sign."

"You may be right, but regardless, just come. Put your differences aside for the trip and join us. Afterward you two can sort things out. Call the agency and book the flight, okay?"

"Okay, I'll book the flight."

"Good!"

The silence lasted for about ten minutes. There was plenty to think about.

"You know you need to work with them, right?" asked the governor, but it was more like a statement. "Dick was just trying to make you think you had a choice, but you really don't. He wanted me to be the one to make that clear to you."

"I just want to work overseas and do my own thing. I don't want those types of strings attached to me. More important than that is that I can't stand being lied to, ever. It drives me wild. If I worked for them, everything would be a lie. I can't live like that."

"Take some time to think it through. Whatever you do, don't call him before we discuss it again. Okay?"

"Okay, I promise," I replied.

After a few moments of silence, the governor spoke.

"I gotta admit, David, I didn't know you had it in you."

"Governor, to be underestimated can be such a beautiful advantage," I replied, with a smug smile.

"Yes, it sure can," replied the governor, also with a smile.

65

AFTER THE PAST two days, only one thing was absolutely certain: I would never return to my cubicle at Lucent Technologies. The days of allowing my soul to be stifled were over. The past few days gave me a taste of what it felt like to be alive. The irony of all this was that it took being at such a low point in my life, questioning my very purpose in this world, for me to be able to connect with my inner self. It was being in sync with my soul that gave me eyes to see that this mystery woman and I were somehow connected or something.

Never could I have imagined that this mystery woman who I now know was Nathalie Rosenfeld and myself shared the same purpose in life, which was to discover Adolf Hitler's deception and his secret plot against America. The universe presented her as an omen that only my eyes could see. Revealing the truth would not have been possible were it not for Nathalie. It was her sacrifice that allowed me to achieve our shared purpose in life. I admired her passion and sense of purpose, and for that I sought to honor her by recovering the duplicate photographs so that Nathalie's father could secure the return of his family's artworks that were stolen by the Nazis.

In this world everything that happens in our lives connects to the past, present, or future. A soul in one time is capable of sending ripples through time and across dimensions. In my dream, the mystery of Nathalie had revealed itself. Our souls had crossed paths in another life a long time ago. Nathalie and I were kindred spirits, and I hoped that the return of her family's stolen artworks would allow her soul to be at peace, until the next time our souls cross paths.

I didn't want to be "the messenger," but my countrymen had a right to know about Hitler's deception. But how will I tell them? A fictional novel, perhaps? It doesn't matter that Hitler's deception is both logical and rational. The cognitive dissonance within the population will never permit them to accept the "Hitler deception" version of World War II history. It would simply be too devastating. Regardless, they still had a right to know the truth; whether or not they choose to believe it is up to them. The whole matter has the potential to get very sensitive, so for that reason it'll be a fictional novel, and I'll paint the work with broad brush strokes and without names; that way if things get too hot, I can distance myself from the theory, just in case.

The events of the previous two days would forever change my life. Given the secrets I had learned, it was thought the only way to keep myself safe was to get under the umbrella of the CIA. Without the protection of the CIA, it was quite likely that I would meet the same fate as Nathalie. Regardless, rather than joining the agency that orchestrated Nathalie's death, I wanted to take my own path, even if it would be at the expense of having to spend the rest of my life looking over my shoulder. *It's a matter of principle*, I thought.

Make the lie big, keep it simple, keep saying it, and eventually they will believe.

—Adolf Hitler

Men occasionally stumble over the truth, but most of them pick themselves up and hurry off as if nothing ever happened.

—Winston Churchill

How fortunate for leaders that men do not think.

—Adolf Hitler

The ruling class has the schools and press under its thumb. This enables them to sway the emotions of the masses.

—Albert Einstein

Part 4

Author's Note

A LOOSE END is a work of fiction. With that said, this book was inspired by an actual event. I witnessed the scene detailed in the opening chapter of this book. I wrote the chapter exactly as it unfolded, except for one detail: after the man handed the mystery woman the brown envelope, as he turned away toward the exit, I could have sworn for a fraction of a second that he made eye contact with me through the reflection in the mirror. Not wanting to confuse the reader, I chose not to include that one detail. After that first chapter, all names, characters, and the storyline are the work of the writer's imagination, and any resemblance to actual persons is entirely coincidental. The historical events mentioned in the book, such as Hitler's ascent, the role of America's corporations in militarizing the Third Reich, details about World War II, the Black Eagle Trust, Operation Paperclip, the Cold War, Continuity of Government (COG) plans, and the Federal Reserve, are all factual. This is the side of history that we aren't taught or hear about but is only learned through deliberate effort.

It was while writing this book that I came up with the "original" Adolf Hitler conspiracy theory—that it was always Hitler's plan to lose World War II. There are countless books that discuss a Nazi Fourth Reich, Hitler's Fifth Column in America, and many other Nazi conspiracies, but I have never come across any theory that it was always Adolf Hitler's plan to lose World War II. This is the part of the theory that is mine, and it came about because of the enigma of Operation Barbarossa, which was Hitler's suicidal decision to invade the Soviet Union. Ever since university, when I first learned about that operation, it just never made any sense to me. I didn't buy that Hitler was crazy. Evil, yes, but that doesn't preclude him from being an evil genius. Being evil and a genius are not mutually exclusive.

The purpose of this book is to allow the reader to learn about Adolf Hitler and the defeat of the Nazis from an alternative perspective to demonstrate how the official version of events is not always consistent with the actual facts.

• • •

About the Author

David Morsilli is the author of *A Loose End*. Before taking time to write this novel, David served with the US Agency for International Development in Afghanistan as part of the civilian surge in 2010. There, he was embedded with the US Marines for Operation Moshtarak, the objective of which was to retake control of the Taliban stronghold of Marjah in Helmand Province.

Prior to that assignment, David worked in the field of humanitarian emergencies for the International Rescue Committee (IRC) in Somalia, where he established the IRC's first field office in the country and implemented water, sanitation, and hygiene projects. Before that he worked with the IRC as camp manager of a camp for internally displaced persons in Darfur.

David also worked for the American Red Cross on the Hurricane Katrina disaster-relief operations. David's first overseas experience came as a Peace Corps volunteer in Macedonia, where he worked on community development projects in the community of Saraj.

In David's first job after completing his liberal arts degree at Boston University, he worked as an aide to Governor Bruce Sundlun of Rhode Island.

David is a native Rhode Islander and currently lives in Providence.

40122193R00154

Made in the USA
Middletown, DE
03 February 2017